REFLECTIONS

CHARLIE KAAR

ISBN: 0692453024
ISBN-13: 978-0692453025

DEDICATION

This book was written for three very important figures in my life. For that fifteen year old girl who promised me when she grew up she would be a woman. For the man who never acknowledged the woman he stared at each morning when he would wake up. And for that somebody who was afraid to admit to the world that they were someone other than what people expected them to be.

CHARLIE KAAR

Food for Thought

When I was a little girl no one ever told me that men were once boys. I just always saw boys and men. I never truly understood the concept. Boys are men in the making and men are grown boys. Boys seek domination. They associate the masculine quality of strength with superiority, and use it negatively. Men realize that the measure of one's strength is not in comparison to another's weakness. They realize that if there WERE to be a real measure of strength, it would probably have something to do with how willing they are to be vulnerable to the things that really matter. No one ever taught me that women were to love men. Well what constitutes a woman? Being a woman is recognition of some of the weaknesses that you may be forced upon you, like periods and the pains of child birth from birth, and the uphill battle you might face in this ever-changing world. It's also recognizing the strengths that come with womanhood. The strength of your heart, your mind, and your body, which differ from woman to woman and culturally being accepted by you and also understood. Being a woman means being strong, because you'll find that your womanhood will need that strength, and when you let it, sometimes that strength will even find you.

If men are to be men and women are to be women, then why is there a shortage of men and women? Are the girls that are supposed to mature to womanhood still waiting for maturity and are the boys sitting at home watching cartoons instead of building strengths as men? I don't know but I do know that love shouldn't be defined by your gender or you choice of spouse. Love doesn't lie, it holds truth. The truth that no one wants to hear and the truth that everyone wants to believe. Love is real.

REFLECTIONS

CONTENTS

CHARLIE KAAR

FLASHBACK

I was born in Orlando, FL on November 21, 1982. My mother had met my father while stationed in Trenton, New Jersey. She had one child (my older brother, Alex) already from a previous marriage. She was married for five years and in her third year of marriage had a child. She divorced Alex's father after coming from a six month tour to him in the bed with another woman. He took custody of Alex since she was enlisted in the service. My father was a construction worker. He was working on a contract on the Jersey Turnpike. He would drive from New York every day to work. Then one day, he was at a bar in Trenton. He saw my mother sitting alone and asked her to dance. Over the next three months, the two went on a series of dates. Then my mother felt nausea one day. She checked herself in the ER and they told her she was pregnant. Nine months later, I was born. The first eight years of my life I lived with my family in Brooklyn, New York. My mother was in the army and she couldn't take me with her, so she left me with my father. My father was a crack addict. He had started using drugs when I was three years old.

CHARLIE KAAR

With his drug problem, my grandmother took me in under her wing. I loved my grandmother. She was so sweet. She potty trained me, taught me how to tie my shoes, ride a bike, my ABC's, my numbers, and how to be a good girl. I was very fond of her. Then when I was six years old, she suffered from a massive stroke. The stroke caused her to have a severe case of amnesia/dementia. The doctors believed she would make it but she would never remember everything in her past. For months, she would wake up and question where she was and who all the people in her house were. My aunts and uncles decided it would be best to put her in a nursing home where she could receive proper treatment.

My father regained custody of me. He made it very clear to me that he didn't want me around. Each day he would come into my room and tell me he was going to work and that he had left food on the stove. There never was food on the stove or anywhere in the house. There were no TVs, furniture (other than my bed), no stove, and no refrigerator in the house. So when my father would wake me, I knew he was lying. I would call my aunt and she would bring me food and take me to school each day. He would leave the house early in the morning and come back late in the evening. When he came home, he always looked and smelled like he hadn't had a bath in years. He received checks from my mother to take care of me. Most of the money was used for drugs.

Even though I was young, I knew that he had a problem. One day my mother called him and told him he would be cut off and I was to move in with my aunt Caroline in Florida. My father was enraged. He came into my room one morning and told me to get all my stuff together because we had to go. I gathered my clothes and put them in a bag. Then we got in the car and just drove and drove.

(Riding in the car with my father on that very hot day)

Daddy where are we going?
We are going to find your mama. I'm sick of her shit.
But daddy I thought....
Hush you know I'm a man and girls must respect men.

THE INITIATION

Chuchie, come on let's go! Everyone is waiting for you. The woman yelled. Sierra I know. I'm almost ready, five more minutes.

Chuchie had a good head on her shoulders after being raised by a great woman and no father. You know the girl that everyone loves but deep inside they can't stand, that was her. She had the whit, the body, the attitude, and the structure. She was the cream de la cream of the city. She had worked so hard and now she was a success.

You said that an hour ago. If you don't come on, we are going to leave you. Her best friend said from downstairs. Ok ok. I'm coming. Chanel yelled back.

Chuchie glanced at herself in the mirror one last time. She knew that this was a lifetime opportunity and she wouldn't miss it for the world.

Now presenting the woman of the hour, the leading lady, and the reason we are all here today. Ms. Chanel Alexander. The announcer announced.

CHARLIE KAAR

Thanks so much for that lovely introduction. First of all, I would like to thank you all for being here. This was once upon a time just a figment of my imagination. I remember many years ago, I said I want to be on top of the world. Here I am today on top of the world. Many of you probably wonder how I got here or what did I do to amount to such success. Well honestly, it started many years ago when I was in an embryo sac. I thank God for such a privilege and it will be an honor to serve you guys. I look forward to a great four years. I'm ready to rebuild Fayetteville. Thank you so much.

After the initiation ceremony Chuchie was ready to relax. Her feet were hurting and all she wanted to do was soak them in Epsom salt and warm water. She pulled into her driveway and turned off the engine. She sat for a second and flashbacks of her younger days flashed in her head. She slowly exhaled and began to get out the car, when suddenly someone called her name from behind her.

Excuse me, are you Mrs. Alexander? Yes I am, who are you and what are you doing at my house? My name is Jamarcus Reed and I'm an editor for Speak Up magazine. Oh right, our interview is tomorrow I thought. She spoke. Yes it is, but I'm so excited that I decided to begin tonight if it is ok with you. He confessed as the woman was in a slight daze. It's fine. Come on in. She said as she unlocked the door to her home.

The two quickly entered into Chuchie's mansion. The lights came on as they entered the house. It was a beautiful home. Chanel knew she had worked hard for this home. Mr. Reed marveled at the mansion. Let me prepare myself and I will give you a tour. For now you can just make yourself at home.

EARLY BEGINNINGS

Chuchie's mother had three children. Alex was the oldest. He was the man of the house. B the baby was spoiled rotten. And Chanel was the middle child better known as the child that was forgotten in her words.

Mama
What?
Umm...
If you don't say what you want right this minute I'm going beat you back to Africa.
Yes ma'am. I was just wondering, does my daddy love me?
Why you ask that?
He never comes to see me or brings me anything like Alex and B's daddy do.
Your daddy is, was, and always will be a fool. One day you will understand.

Toga and Ce Ce were Chuchie's best friends in middle and high school. Toga was fat light skin and really mischievous. He was always up to no good. Ce Ce was a pretty chocolate complexion girl. Her and Chuchie knew each other since diapers. Their families were both of the Jehovah's witness faith.

CHARLIE KAAR

Toga, come on before we get caught. Chanel said in fear of the worse. Nobody gone see us. We just looking anyways. The young man said to calm the fearful Chanel. If they catch us I'm going leave you. You know you can't run. Chanel confessed as the boy tried to figure out they were about to commit this crime.

Ha ha ha, Ce Ce laughed. What you laughing at? That's why you ugly. You ugly and that's why y'all have to go to church every day. Y'all can't even celebrate holidays. Toga iterated. Shut up Toga and Ce Ce. Chuchie said in rage.

Toga jumped the fence and stood for a second. Then he started to run towards the house. The house was Ms. Kitley's house. Her husband had passed a few years back and now she was senile.

We going take the bikes and leave out the back fence. If you get caught say you didn't know no better and you were going to bring it back. Toga spoke as he prepared to hop the fence of the cage where the bikes were. This is stupid. Ce Ce said as she stared at the unmoved leader. Why can't we just ask for the bikes? Chanel puzzled as she stared at the old house. Shut up and let's do this. Toga yelled as he jumped the fence.

It was only nine o clock and all of us had to be home by ten. Toga spotted the bike he wanted. It was black with white stripes across the bars. He quickly walked over to it and hopped on it. Ce Ce and Chuchie followed. They took the bikes and parked them in back of Chuchie's house since her mom was the nicest.

Chuchie, are you asleep? Ce Ce asked as she leaned over her best friend. No. Chuchie replied as she pushed her friend away from her.

Do you think that we will get in trouble for taking those bikes today? Ce Ce puzzled as she scooted closer to Chanel. No I think she won't even notice they are gone. Chanel said. True. Why are you not asleep? Ce Ce asked. Cause you hoggin all the covers. Chanel answered angrily. Well come get some. Ce Ce said as she nudged her friends arm. What? Chanel asked. Want to play a game? Ce Ce thought out loud. Not really. What's the game? Chanel said as she turned over and now faced her friend in the dark. Play house. Ce Ce answered. What is that? I never heard of that before. Chanel spoke. You have to take all your clothes and me too. Whoever gets them off the fastest wins. The loser has to walk outside naked or lick the other person's butt. Ce Ce explained. Ha ha ha. That's stupid. Chanel joked.

REFLECTIONS

It was pitch black in the house. Chuchie's aunt had been sleep for hours. Her and her best friend lay in the bed together for a sleepover.

Alright I'll play. Chanel said as she prepared to play the game. Ok on three ready set three. Ce Ce whispered. The two rushed to get their clothes off. Chuchie got hers off first. So which you wanna do? Your choice. Ha ha ha. Chanel joked as she now sat up on the bed naked. Do you want me to touch you? Ce Ce asked as she sat up next to her. I don't care. Chanel answered as she felt Ce Ce's cold hand touch her leg.

The two began kissing slowly and the girl went down slowly embracing Chuchie's body. She was only ten years old. This was her first time ever having someone else touch her. She didn't know what she was feeling but she knew she liked it.

The three amigos grew up together. They attended Saint Paul Elementary School. Then, later attended Bulin High School; up until Toga got expelled for setting the bathroom on fire. Ce Ce was the smartest person Chuchie knew. She would make straight A's in school. Chuchie was very smart as well but she settled for being a B student.

Toga didn't care about anything. He stayed in trouble. Chanel had said that Toga got in trouble so much because he missed his father. When Toga was twelve, his father was murdered. That left him and his mother alone. His mother was forced to work thee jobs to take care of him and her. She was never home with him. Each holiday he would be given gifts right before his mom went to work.

Hey pretty lady. He spoke as he stared her up and down. Hi Mikey! She said unmoved. So what's up? He asked touching her back. She pulled away as she waited for Toga to pick her up.

Mikey was smooth. He was a fair skinned, handsome, and educated brother. Chuchie was enticed by him but she knew he was nothing but trouble. He was dating Theresa at the time. She was one of Ce Ce's teammates. They played soccer together.

CHARLIE KAAR

Why don't I have your number? Mikey puzzled. Because you never asked for it. Chanel spoke. So what is it? He asked. 850 jump off a cliff. She joked. Why you gotta be so mean? He asked as he was now staring at her booty. You know you want me. He finished as she turned away. I do not. You have the big head. I'm not ever in life gonna be with you. Get that through your head. She raged. Why? Am I not good enough for you? He said as he pulled her closer to him. Exactly, you are too good to be true. She spoke as she pushed him away from her. You are very delicate I would never do anything to hurt you. Give me a chance please! He said as she walked closer to the curve. Bye Mikey. She said as a car pulled up.

Toga finally pulled up. She quickly got into the car. What took you so long? Chanel raged. I have something I have to tell you Chanel. He said as he sped off. What is it? Chanel puzzled. We will talk about it at my house. He said as he turned on the radio. Chanel just sat back and enjoyed the ride. She wondered what he was about to tell her.

He finally pulled into his driveway. His mom was at work as usual. He got out the car and walked over to open Chuchie's door. Thanks Toga. She said as she got out the car. Yea, you're welcome. He said as he walked onto the porch. She followed behind him. He opened the door and the two entered the house.

Mrs. Jackson's at work? Chanel puzzled as she walked in and sat on the sofa. The house was very neat and tidy. Toga always made sure the house was clean. He said it was the least he could do since his mom was always working. Yea, she should be here in a bit. He said as he walked into the kitchen. Do you want anything to eat? He yelled as he stood staring in the fridge. No thank you. Chanel replied as she walked in the kitchen. So what you have to tell me? Chanel asked as she sat on the counter.

Toga wasn't afraid of anything. After his father had died, he seemed to not fear anything. He got involved with a gang. He stayed in trouble in school and he always had a few crazy girlfriends in his life. On that day, Toga had fear in his eyes. He was very afraid to tell Chanel the truth.

I have a baby on the way. He said as he moved closer to her. Chanel was in love with Toga. She loved the way he treated her and all other females, she loved how brave he was, and she loved how he could fix anything with his bare hands. She had believed in her heart that the two would end up getting married and having several children.

REFLECTIONS

You what? Chanel asked in disbelief. Robyn is pregnant and she said she wants to keep it. He said. Robyn was Toga's stupid girlfriend. The only thing she had going for herself was her looks. She was about 5'6, with short curly hair, and a body shaped like a coke bottle. She and Toga had been dating for six months. Chanel really hated her guts.

I can't believe you could be so dumb Toga. Chanel said with a tear in her eye. I'm not good enough for you and I never will be. Toga said as he stood in between Chanel's legs as she sat on the counter. Whatever! How do you know what's good for me? Chanel asked as she tried to push him from in between her legs. You and Ce Ce have a way out. I'm going be stuck in the streets the rest of my life. I can't be with you in that. He confessed. But you can be with her and get her pregnant? Chanel spoke furiously.

I love you enough to keep you from falling like that. Now her life is ruined forever because I may not be able to see my kids grow up. He said as he pushed his face into Chanel's chest. I don't care. Chanel said as her eyes were blood shot red from crying. I'm going home. She said as she pushed him away from her and hopped off the counter.

He chased after her as she headed towards the door. He grabbed her arm and pulled her to face him. He now stood with her in his grip. She didn't bother to resist as he began to kiss her neck. Toga was now a man and Chanel was still a girl. He had lost the extra weight from his childhood as he got older. Chanel was in love with a man.

I love you. He said to her as he licked her neck. I love you too, she said holding back tears. He licked her ears one by one. Then he picked her up and took her into his bedroom. She held on as if she knew what was about to happen. He slowly shut the door with his foot as he held her like she was a damsel in distress. He placed her down on his bed. She sat up staring at him as he took off his clothes.

Are you afraid? He asked as he now stood naked in front of her. No, she replied. He moved closer to her. He leaned her back on the bed and began to undress her. Is this what you want to do? He asked as he finally got all her clothes off. Yes, I've waited for this moment for a very long time. I wanted you to be my first and last. She spoke as tear rolled down her left cheek. He wiped her tear from her face with his tongue.

He slowly began to lick her all over. She squirmed in satisfaction. He then began sticking his tongue in and out of her mouth. Come on and suck on it for a minute. He said as he pulled her on top of him. He now was solid as a rock. Chanel first looked at his manhood. She didn't know what to do. She thought this is too big to put into my mouth. She began to lick it side to side and from top to bottom. She could tell he liked it by the way he was moaning.

After a few minutes of her sucking on him, he wanted to be inside of her. Alright get on top. He said as he pulled her up. He slowly tried to ease inside of her as she sat on top of him. Ouch Ouch! She yelled in pain. He sat up and put her down on the bed. She was now lying on her back. You just have to relax and let me in. He said as he kissed her neck. He pulled her closer into his arms. She wrapped her legs around him as he pushed deeper and deeper. He finally got in. He started going crazy. He stroked her harder and harder as she moaned. He flipped her over on her stomach and began pumping inside of her. She moaned louder and louder.

He pumped in and out of her for about thirty minutes. He then pulled out and came all over her back. How do you feel? He asked as wiped his mess clean from her back. I don't know. Chanel spoke. I just want you to know I love you Chanel and to never let a man come in between what you have and what you love. He said before turning over and going to sleep.

Chanel left the house as he was sleeping. She had just lost her virginity to the man she loved but she didn't feel as happy as she thought she would. Her vagina was throbbing. It felt she had been getting punched in it none stop for the past two hours. All she wanted to do was take a shower and lie down.

Three days later, Chuchie was finally feeling better. She invited her best friend over to spend a night. She wanted to invite Toga but she knew it wasn't right. He would just want to have sex with me played over and over again her head. She knew she had to tell Ce Ce before Toga told her.

Ce Ce arrived at her house around 8:30 that night. The two stayed up watching movies and eating junk food. So I lost my virginity. Chanel confessed as Ce Ce sat on the floor eating chips. What? When did this happen? Ce Ce puzzled. Three days ago. It wasn't perfect at all. Chanel spoke as she lay across her bed. Who took it? Ce Ce asked as she passed the chips to Chuchie. Chanel didn't want to tell her. She didn't want her judging her.

REFLECTIONS

Toga! Chanel said trying not to look Ce Ce in her eyes. What? No way? Ce Ce said as she hopped on the bed. Yea, we did it. Chanel said scooting away from her. How did it happen? Ce Ce puzzled staring her in the eyes. It was long and hard. Chanel said as she turned her head. Well I know that, but… Ce Ce started. What do you mean you know that? Chanel cut her off. I'm saying I know it was painful. Ce Ce spoke as Chanel eyed her. I hope you didn't think I was saying I wanted Toga. That's nasty. She finished.

Don't tell anyone or I will kill you. Chanel said as she sat up on the bed. I won't. I have a secret too. Ce Ce said as she sat up as well. Do you promise to never tell? Ce Ce asked. Of course, now tell me. Chanel rushed. I'm a lesbian. Ce Ce confessed. What? That's the big secret? I already knew Ce Ce. Chanel said as she lay back down. How? Ce Ce quizzed staring in disbelief. You never had a boyfriend in your life and every guy that ever tried to talk to you, you denied. Chanel said still unmoved. But you can't tell anyone. Ce Ce said worried. I never did and never will. Chanel confirmed.

THAT GUY

My curiosity excited me when he walked pass. He stared at me for a second and I almost fainted. He is so fine girl. Kim said as she stared at the guy in the line. You should go and talk to him. Stacy spoke as he walked away with his food. No, for what? He's just like all the rest of them. Chanel said before leaving.

Stacy and Kim were Chuchie's roommates back in college. Stacy was Italian and Kim was mixed with white and black. Kim resembled Mya and Stacy resembled the average white girl (no ass and huge tits). The three met at a freshmen mixer at Soli Forum University.

Chuchie sat in the library with her laptop studying for her pysch midterm. She sipped on a caramel latte and jammed to her Lauryn Hill CD.

Excuse me. He said as he walked up to her and tapped her on the shoulder. Yes? She answered removing her headphones. I know Lauryn is the best, but can you turn your music down. He asked as he pointed at the CD player. No way! She responded. The two just laughed. How rude of me? I'm Tony. He said as reached for her hands. I'm Chanel. She replied. So what is your major? She puzzled as he grabbed a chair and sat down. Psychology, you? He questioned as he glared at her beauty. History, she answered. Wow, I would have never guessed. He said in disbelief. I love history. It repeats itself if you don't know how and what happened. She confessed.

REFLECTIONS

The two sat and talked about history and psychology for about thirty minutes. The conversation made Chuchie feel something deep inside. She liked his intellect on life and the way he talked. She now liked the way he looked and thought. She had seen him every day for the past six months and now he sat next to her talking. God works in mysterious ways.

It was really nice to talk to you. Maybe some time we can hang out. He said as he began to get up from his chair. Ok I'll see you around. Chanel said as he walked away.

Tony?
Yea.
Why me?
What you mean?
Of all the other girls you could be hanging out with on a beautiful Friday night, you are here with me.
I want you.
What does that mean?
I think you are a very special lady. And I needed a date to show to the homies.

The two laughed. As they approached the lounge, Chuchie's heart began to race. She hadn't been here in such a long time.

So you like poetry right? He asked as they stood under a light pole. I love poetry. She responded as she wrapped her arms around the back of his neck. I'm going to recite some poetry tonight and I want you to critique me. He spoke as he kissed her cheeks.

They entered the lounge. Tony showed her to her seat and then he was off to the back. Performer after performer, Chuchie awaited Tony's performance. Then finally the host announced him.

WITHOUT BREATH THERE IS NO LIFE
WITHOUT THE SUN, THE PLANTS AND THE OCEANS
FADE AND DIE
WITH ESSENCE COMES PRIDE
BUT WITH ART A BEAUTY IS SOON TO ARISE
A WOMAN IT'S IN HER HEART AND A MAN YOU CAN
SEE IT IN HIS EYES
IT'S LIKE ZION THE MOST HIGH
THE SECRET FORMATION OF LOVE THAT BUILDS
DEEP INSIDE
IT STARTS WITH A HEY AND NEVER REACHES A BYE
A BLISSFUL JOY COMING ON DEEP IN THE NIGHT
IT NEVER EVER LEAVES EVEN AFTER BEING
PROLAPSED FOR A LONG TIME
IT JUST SITS AND WAITS FOR ITS TIME TO SHINE
A GIFT FROM GOD THAT IS GIVEN TO BOTH YOU AND I
THIS PECULIAR STATE OF MIND
THAT GIVES YOU CHILLS UP AND DOWN YOUR SPINE
THOSE WHO WONDER WHY
HAVE TO REALIZE
LOVE IS ART THAT KILLS YOU BUT LETS YOU SURVIVE

His words were so thoughtful and creative she thought as he walked off stage.

SERENAI

That was so beautiful Tony. Chanel said as she kissed him. Thanks, I wrote it for you. He said as the two began to sit down. Really? She puzzled as she stared at the man she was in love with. Yes, you are the most beautiful woman I ever met in my life. And I know we have only been seeing each other for a year now but I know that this is real. You are the person that I see myself spending the rest of my life with. So Ms. Chanel... He started.

Chuchie, OMG what are you doing here? Serenai interrupted. OMG, Serenai how are you? Chanel said as she stood to hug Serenai. I haven't seen you in here in ages. I'm doing pretty well. She spoke as the two hugged each other. That is great. I read the book. It was beautiful. Chanel confessed. Thanks and who is this handsome, young man with the flow of Gab? Serenai asked as Tony sat staring at the two women. This is my boyfriend Tony. Chanel said remembering Tony was there.

Tony and Serenai shook hands. Tony sensed awkwardness between the two. What Chuchie never told Tony about was her relationship with Serenai. Serenai and Chuchie had met her freshmen year. She had gone to The Flask with her best friend.

The Flask was a lounge that offered many different art forms. The club had a monthly poetry night, a monthly women's seminar, a jazz concert every 3rd Saturday of each month, a rock concert on the 1st Saturday of each month, and an annual pride weekend. Chuchie's freshmen year of college, Sierra came to visit for annual pride weekend. The two decided to go to The Flask.

CHARLIE KAAR

Chuchie was a bit skeptical about hanging out with a gay crowd. Sierra convinced her it would be fun and that she needed her support. So she went along. They were enjoying the music and dancing the night away when it was time for the poetry segment of the night. Many different poets performed both male and female. Then the final poet got on stage. She was fair skinned with long beautiful black hair. Her smile was sparkling white and her eyes were hazel. She had a Hindu bracelet tattoo around her right arm. She was at the most 145lbs and 5'6. She looked like she belonged on a runway.

That's Serenai. You are going to love her. Ce Ce said as the crowd cheered. What? Chanel asked as she looked around the room and noticed her surroundings. She is the best poet in the LGBT community. Ce Ce said as she sipped on her drink. Really, that's cool I guess. Chuchie shrugged. You guess. Just wait for it. You will see.Ce Ce said. Is she... Chanel started. Yes she is a lesbian. Ce Ce said staring at Chanel as if she could slap her for the last comment she had just made. Oh I don't care. Chanel said noticing Ce Ce's face. Why are you always discriminating because of a person's cultural beliefs? Ce Ce puzzled furiously. I'm not. Let's just enjoy the show. Chanel said as the woman walked on stage.

My passion burned deep deep inside
Shrieking sounds from me cried
And no one could ever know this pain I had to hide
He bit my lip kissed my chips and we multiplied
Then he showed me how to add subtract and divide
He taught me how to survive
We were criminals in the day making money in every way and lovers in the night time
Why did I ever commit such a crime
Pushing away my feelings of intuition and pride
Because of him vengeance lives today and love has died

REFLECTIONS

The woman began walking around the room greeting everyone. She made her way to back of the club. Ce Ce swarmed her like a groupie. It' my friends first time here tonight. Ce Ce said as she pulled Serenai to where Chanel and she had been standing all night. The woman spotted Chanel. This is Serenai Chuchie. Ce Ce said as they reached her. That was so beautiful. I am such a huge fan. Chuchie said to the woman. Stop. You're making me blush. Serenai joked.

Chuchie was a huge fan of Serenai. Her words spoke to her in so many ways. She was also a highly, cultured person. She could speak English, Spanish, and Italian.

So are the rumors true? Chanel asked as Ce Ce left to dance with a girl. Well it all depends on what they are saying about me. Tell me. Serenai whispered into her ear. You're a lesbian, right? Chanel asked as she backed away. I consider myself to be a rose. A rose is merely a gift to those who cherish her. But if you don't, petal by petal I will leave your side. Serenai explained as the music roared.
I'm not interested or nothing. I was just saying. I don't like girls. Chanel claimed. Curiosity kills the cat. Serenai whispered. I know. Chanel replied now disgusted.

The two talked for what seemed like hours as Ce Ce danced. Serenai listened as Chuchie talked about school. She explained her major and why she had chosen it. She talked about her favorite professor and how she had a huge crush on him. Serenai talked about the places she had traveled to and the places she wanted to go to.

Chuchie are you ready to go? Ce Ce asked as she returned from the dance floor. Yea sure, I'm ready. Chanel said as she began getting up from her seat. I hope to see you again someday Ms. Chanel. Here's my number, give me a call. Serenai said with her hand stretched out. Thanks. Goodbye. Chanel said as she took the card.

Serenai likes you Chanel. Ce Ce said as the two walked out of the club. What? Chuchie questioned. She likes you. Ce Ce stated. How do you know? Chuchie asked yearning for more. The way she looks at you, Sierra informed. Ok If you say so lesbian. Chuchie joked. You are very beautiful and she noticed. Sierra told Chuchie.

Hey this is Chuchie, I mean Chanel. We met at pride weekend. Chanel said nervously. She wondered if it was the right thing to do.

Oh hey, I've been thinking about you. Serenai said as she realized who it was. Ok, cool. Chanel brushed it off. What are you doing tonight? Serenai puzzled. Laundry, Chanel replied.

Ok come out with me tonight. The grand opening of the new art gallery downtown is tonight. They are featuring a few of my pieces so I will be in attendance. Serenai said. Sure I would love to go. Chanel gleamed. Ok I'll pick you up at eight from Chalin Hall. Serenai said. Ok see you then. Chanel said before hanging up the phone.

Chuchie didn't know what she was to do. She was a bit confused. She had a small feeling inside her telling her that she liked Serenai. Then her mind was telling her no. So she looked for the best outfit she could find in her closet. She found her black velvet dress. She had only previously worn the dress once to her high school graduation.

Where are you going? Kim questioned as she walked into Chuchie's room. I'm going to the Grand Opening of Libe' de Cult downtown. Chuchie answered proudly. Cool, so you and Sham going on a romantic date again? No, I'm going with Serenai.

Kim was from Baton Rouge, Louisiana. She was the only child until she was sixteen and her mother had a son from her second marriage. Kim lived with her father. Her father was a financial consultant. His family owned three different offices. One was in Baton Rouge, one was in Detroit, and one was in Los Angeles. The Alon family were millionaires before Kim was born. She was a pampered princess. Everything she asked for she received. While growing up, she was raised in the Jewish faith. She didn't believe in Jesus and homosexuality was blasphemy in her eyes.

Isn't she a lesbian? Kim quizzed Chanel. I don't know and really don't care. Chuchie answered. If you hang out with her she is going to turn you out. Kim enforced. Turn me out? My best friend is gay and has been for years. I think I would be gay already if I could be turned. Chuchie stated. Listen, she's different. Trust me I know... Kim reiterated. What do you mean? Chuchie questioned.
We used to date.

REFLECTIONS

Kim and Serenai had met at Paris. Paris was a small night club downtown. She had gone to go hang out with a group of friends. While dancing a woman walked up to her and asked her if she wanted to dance. She said yes and the two danced all night. Kim was wearing blue mini shorts, a black t-shirt, and some red heels. Her hair was naturally curly, long, and pretty. Her skinned glowed and her eyes were blue. She was beautiful.

So what's your name? Kim whispered in the woman's ear. Serenai, what's yours? Serenai asked. I'm Kim. I'm a student at Soli Forum University. Kim responded as she continued to dance. Cool. So where are you from? Serenai asked noticing Kim's body. Baton Rouge. Kim answered. The music echoed as the two continued their conversation. How about we go have some coffee so we can talk with a little less noise? Serenai whispered in her ear. Sure let's go. Kim responded.

The two fell in love over coffee. Serenai loved Kim's confidence and Kim loved Serenai's charisma. The two almost broke up after Kim's father told her she would be cut off from her inheritance if she didn't get her act together. Kim told her father she was in love with Serenai and they would spend the rest of their lives together. Then Kim's grandmother passed and her father blamed her passing on Kim. He said she had died from a broken heart about Kim's lifestyle choices. Kim couldn't take it anymore so she told Serenai they couldn't be together anymore. They dated for ten months.

I'm not into girls. Chanel said as she pulled clothes out of her dresser. I wasn't either. I'm warning you. She strikes like a cobra. Kim said moving as Chuchie threw clothes all over the place. What? I'm not into girls. You know I love Sham. Chanel said as she looked at herself in the mirror. Yea, just be careful ok? Kim spoke. Yea sure! Thanks for looking out. Chanel said as she hugged Kim. No problemo. Kim said before leaving the room

CHARLIE KAAR

Chuchie slowly walked down the sidewalk. Her dreads were now pinned in a style. She wore six inch, open toe black heels, her nails were neatly polished with blue polish, her lips were lightly painted with lip gloss, she carried a black leather tote in her right hand, and she wore a black velvet dress that was just a little above her knees. The dress helped show her curves. She was a dark complexioned girl. She was quite the looker.

As she approached Chalin Hall, she noticed a small blue car at the far left of the building. The car began to move towards her. She noticed Serenai was driving. She quickly rushed to the car, grabbed the door, and jumped in. The two both sat in silence the entire ride. Neither spoke to one another. The car drove for what seemed to be an hour until it reached the gallery.

Serenai drove to the back of the gallery and parked in a space that said reserved. Then she got out of the car and walked over to the passenger side to open Chuchie's door. Chuchie slowly stepped out. Serenai held out her arm signaling Chuchie to grab it. Chuchie wrapped her arm in Serenai's and the two headed for the door. As they approached the door, Chuchie noticed the words *We Welcome All Who Enjoy*. She wondered what that meant.

The two of them together were beautiful. Chuchie was the black beauty and Serenai was white beauty. Serenai had her hair in long, beautiful curls. Her lips were painted with red lipstick to embrace her light skin tone. Her nails, fingers and toes, were painted red to embrace her lipstick. Her eyebrows were neatly arched. Right below her left nostril and a little to the right, she had a small beauty mark. She wore ruby earrings. She had on a long white gown. The gown had a deep ripple on the right side, no sleeves, and was backless. She was wearing a pair of crème white heels that were covered by the length of the dress. She was fabulous.

The two walked around the gallery looking at each piece of art. At each piece of art, both would describe what they saw, felt, and believed it to be. After they had walked and saw almost all of the pieces, the two finally reached a piece of Serenai's. Serenai quickly began to smile. She knew that it would impress Chuchie.

This is my favorite piece in the entire gallery. It represents a greater meaning. Serenai joked.

Chuchie quickly began to read the piece. It read

REFLECTIONS

LOVE TICKLES THE SOUL
SCARES THE HEART
AND BREAKS THE MOLD
FOOLISH LUST AND WEARY EYES
THIS LOVE LEAVES US BLIND
REACHING FOR WHATEVER IT CAN HOLD ONTO
NOT REALIZING THE TRUTH
FOLLY MEN BESEECH THEMSELVES
NOT ACCEPTING ANY HELP
SO LOVE IS LEFT
NOW IT'S THE BLAME AND HAS A BAD REP

Wow! This is really great.

Thanks.

I think your words are so beautiful. You should definitely think about doing a book.

I never really planned on doing a book.

Why? It could be nice.

Right could be. I don't know for sure if it will work.

To whom much is given much is expected. If you don't write, your purpose is not going to be accomplished.

I'll think about it.

SERENAI'S PAST

Serenai had never had anyone to encourage her. She was a foster child of the city of Detroit. By the age of fifteen, she had been with ten different families. Her mother was diagnosed with cancer and had died when Serenai was two. None of Serenai's aunts or uncles wanted her, so she was placed in foster care. At first she was a good child, but by the age of ten she was called The Demon Child by the department of children and families. She tortured her brothers and sisters in each foster home. She stole from corner stores. She set trashcans on fire in different neighborhoods. She once buried the family cat in the backyard while it was still alive. By high school, she liked to skip school. She would skip school to get high or to have sex with her then boyfriend, Frank. The two would skip school just to have sex.

REFLECTIONS

Frank was also in foster care. He was a bad influence on Serenai. He taught her how to smoke, steal, gamble, and how to cause complete havoc. He trained her to survive as the lowest of the low. He told her that in order for her to stay alive, she would have to fight for what was hers all the time. Serenai loved Frank. He was the only person she believed understood what she was going through.

His father and mother were both crack heads when they met. His mother, Rachel, joined a church, cleaned up her life, and got saved. His father, John, later joined the church, got cleaned up, and got a job at a construction site. He first met Rachel during A Better Life with Christ program. It was program for people with drug, alcohol, or sex abuse habits. The two began dating and pushing and encouraging each other to stop using drugs. Then one day, His father decided he would ask Rachel's father for his blessing. Her father granted him the opportunity, so three weeks later she said yes. The two married and in their second year of marriage, Rachel got pregnant with Frank.

John began secretly using drugs again. He lost his job due to always being late and high on the job. So John returned to his street life. He would get up each morning and pretend to be going to a construction site. John was a pimp. He would sell women to make enough money to keep a house over his family's head. He always cheated on Rachel with many women.

Then one day he met a male who came looking to buy a male. John didn't pimp men, he only pimped women. The man offered John $500 to let him have sex with him. John accepted the offer, so the two went to a dark alley. The man told John to drop his pants. He began unbuckling his pants when the man just pulled his pants off. He told John he wasn't hard yet so he had to suck him up first. John sucked on him for about ten minutes, and then the man told him to turn around. He began to lick John's butthole. John moaned loudly. Then the man quickly inserted his shaft in John's butthole. It's so tight man. I love this shit. I'm going come all in your ass and make you scream my name. The man told John as he fucked him. He pumped his butt for hours and hours in the back of the alley. He put his fingers in John's mouth and made him suck them as he pumped him faster and faster.

You want this in your ass?
Yes, put it in my ass.
Beg for it.

CHARLIE KAAR

Give it to me. I want your nut Daddy.

Soon as John finished his sentence, the man came in his butt. John liked the feeling. He had never had sex with a man before, but really liked it.

John began living a double life and eventually started a partnership. Him and his lover Roy would be together in the nights. Roy never knew about John's family. When John would leave, he just thought that he was living with his mother. John had contracted HIV from Roy and didn't know it. He didn't tell his wife of four years, Rachel, that he was on the down low. Then one day she fell ill. She was so sick and no one understood. Frank was only two years old when his mom had first got sick. Then one day the doctor's told her she had AIDS and she only had three months to live. She finally passed when Frank was five years old and his father had a relapse and tried to sell Frank for drugs. The city took him into custody and placed him in foster care.

You have the best pussy I ever had. He said as he stroked her. Yea! She said as he pushed in slower and slower. Yea, your pussy is so much better than Keisha's. He said as he was getting deeper and deeper.

Get off of me, you asshole. She quickly demanded as she pushed Frank off her. What's wrong baby? Frank asked with his dick hanging out. As Serenai put on her clothes she questioned, are you fucking Keisha? No I was back in the day. He answered. You are lying. I knew it. Don't ever call me again. She yelled as she slammed the door behind her.

SHAM

Ugh ugh the moans rung through the ceilings.

Wait. Maybe we should slow down.
Why baby?
I've never done this before.
It's okay.
I know but my my...
Your what? We are just having fun.
 Of course. I just know this is wrong.
Do you want to do this?
 I don't know. I think so.
So just relax, if it was wrong it wouldn't be happening. Everything
happens for a reason.

CHARLIE KAAR

Sham and Chuchie had been dating for two years. She was a freshman and had just moved on campus. She met him in a department store looking for a shower rack during her senior year in high school. He was white boy who wanted to be black. He was two years older than her. He was very afraid of commitment and being with a black girl. His family never approved of his relationship with Chuchie. They claimed they weren't racist, they just were traditional and dating anyone outside of the Jewish community was unacceptable. He never committed to her. He always cheated on her with other girls and he would sell drugs. Chuchie one day got sick of him and she told him she was leaving him.

Why can't you understand baby? I love you more than I love my mama. And you know I love my mama. Sham said as Chanel packed all his things in a box. Whatever! You are not man enough for me. She was furious. I promise I will do better just don't leave me. Sham begged on his knees. One last chance and I have to move on. I'm trying to do better for myself and you are not even trying. She said as he held onto her legs. I promise I can be the man you need. He said as he stood up.

Sham got a job at a consulting firm. He started taking anger management classes and he started looking into investments. He was really turning his life around. Chuchie saw the change and she was really happy that she gave him a second chance.

Then one day, Sham decided to borrow money from Troy. He needed the money to buy Chuchie an engagement ring is what he told Troy. Troy was moved by his story so he loaned him $30,000 and told him he had six months to pay him back $40,000. He agreed to the terms. Sham bought Chuchie a $12,000 ring and used the rest of the money to buy them a small house. He put it in her name. The time finally came for him to ask her to marry her. He decided he had to do it the traditional way. So he made reservations at the Monte Carlo. It was the most upscale restaurant in all of Virginia Beach. But on this night, Chuchie would have to cancel to study for her upcoming finals. Sham forgot to pay Troy back. He had got so caught up in making everything perfect for Chuchie. So Troy sought his revenge.

I promise I won't hurt you if you tell me where he is.
I don't know where he is.

REFLECTIONS

You are his girlfriend right?
Yea but..
But nothing.

Troy was a thug. He sold drugs, robbed, killed, or did whatever he had to. Chuchie didn't realize how crazy he really was.

Please. Let me go. I won't tell.
Shut up.

ugh no.

He raped her and peed on her for five days straight in an old abandoned building. He kidnapped her one day while she was taking out the trash.

Well since your boyfriend can't pay me, I'm gonna kill you. Just like that she was laying in a pool full of blood. He shot her in the stomach and left her to die. A leasing agent found her when he went to do an inspection of the property two days later.

Not my baby. I told her bout them thugs. Her mother thought as she sat patiently in the hospital waiting room. She had been contacted by the police three days ago. She was at home in Orlando, Florida. She immediately got on plane and rushed to her oldest daughter's side. She had begged her mother to let her go to school out of state. Her mother warned her that it was too dangerous. Chuchie didn't want to stay in Florida to go to school.

She knew that the best schools in the country were upstate. She had picked Soli Forum University, a small liberal arts school as her second choice. Threshton was her first. Threshton was $35,000 a year and they only offered her $10,000. Soli Forum University offered a full ride academic scholarship, so she accepted. Her mother approved of it, since she wouldn't have to pay for her daughter's education. Now her mother sat wishing she had never allowed her daughter to leave her home.

CHARLIE KAAR

Hi, I am Dr. Tezeme. Your daughter was rushed to an emergency surgery to remove a bullet a day ago. She was shot in the stomach and the bullet grazed two of her major arteries. She lost a lot of blood. We are doing all we can to help save your daughter's life. Please be patient with us. A woman said as she approached Chuchie's mother.

Thanks Dr. She responded. Hi, Ms. Jones. I am Sergeant Relezes with the Virginia Beach Police Department and I have a few questions for you about your daughter. A woman said as she walked over to Ms. Jones. Ok. Do you guys know who did this to my daughter? The woman puzzled still in shock. No information has been discovered. Was your daughter in any trouble? Relezes aked. No my daughter is a good girl. She came here to get an education and got shot. She could have stayed home for that. Ms. Jones whined. Ma'am, I will do everything in my power to help your daughter. The office said.

Sham suddenly stormed in the emergency room. His face was as red as a stop sign. He walked right over to Ms. Jones. He reached to give her a hug and she quickly pulled away.

Don't you dare touch me boy. I know you had something to do with this. Ms. Jones said as she pulled away from him. I would never hurt your daughter. I love her and want to spend the rest of my life with her. He said with tears rolling down his cheek.

Who are you sir? Sgt. quickly interrupted. I am Chanel's boyfriend. He replied. Ok I am Sergeant Relezes. Why are you just showing up to the hospital? The officer puzzled. We have been here for hours; do you even care about my daughter? Ms. Jones cried. I was in LA on a business trip. I got here as quick as I could. Can we see her? I need to see her. He questioned.

Chuchie: Ugh
Sham: Hey baby, who did this to you?
Ms. Jones: Shut up you heathen! I told my daughter to stay away from your white trash ass.
Sham: I love her and I'm going to do everything I can to fix this.
Chuchie: Sham, baby?
Sham: Who did this to you?

REFLECTIONS

Tears rolled down Chuchie's cheeks. She didn't know whether she should tell or to lie. Troy, she replied in tears. Sham immediately stormed off.

Two weeks after Chuchie was shot, Troy was found dead behind a dumpster. A gun was found at the scene with Sham's fingerprints all over it. He was sentenced to life in prison with no parole. Serenai had been in San Francisco on a business trip. She rushed home as fast as she could to get back to Chuchie.

SHE COULD BE THE ONE

Hey, how are you? Serenai questioned Chuchie as she stroked her hair and kissed her cheeks. Chuchie didn't respond she just smiled. Each day for a month, Serenai went to the hospital to see Chuchie and bring her class work. Chuchie had asked her to go the university and speak with her professors on her behalf. They worked out a way for her to recover and do her work at the same time. After three months in the hospital, Chuchie checked herself out and returned to her house.

Serenai: Are you sure this is what you want?
Chuchie: Yes, I can't be with you anymore. I want children and a family one day. I can't have that with a woman.
Serenai: We could have whatever you wanted.
Chuchie: No we couldn't. You are a woman and I am a woman. There's no such thing possible. It would be a figment of our imaginations.
Serenai: I'm sorry you feel this way. I love you and I always will.

I'M STILL IN LOVE

The two had dated for a year and a half up until she met Tony. When she met Tony she saw him from a distance. He was very attractive to her, but she was in a relationship with Serenai. Kim and Stacy urged her to break up with Serenai several times. Kim told her she knew it was going to happen and Stacy told her she could never have a real family with Serenai. Each day she would defend her relationship with Serenai.

Serenai was perfect. She waited on Chuchie hand and foot. She gave her nice things even when she didn't ask for them. She took her on expensive trips. She was there for her after she got shot. She helped her with her classes and she helped her to get a job at a bank. Serenai was all that she could ever ask for plus more.

Then now at this moment in her life here Serenai was again. She was now a senior in college and in a relationship with Tony. She was now deep in love with Tony. But seeing Serenai somehow made her feel reminiscent about their past relationship. She wondered if they could have ever worked.

Serenai: How are you doing?
Tony: It's nice to meet you.
Serenai:The pleasure is mine. So how about you guys join me at my booth?
Tony: Sure thing. Would you like to sit with your friend baby?
Chuchie: Sure, let's go.

The three began to walk towards the back near a section of booths. Serenai showed them to her booth and told them she would be right back.

Serenai: Can you bring me your best bottle of wine in a bucket of ice and three glasses please?
Hostess: Sure thing madam.

Serenai hadn't seen Chuchie in two years. She was still madly in love with her. She knew that the two of them would meet up again, but this time she promised herself she would not let her go. Serenai slowly glided back to her booth where Chuchie and Tony sat patiently waiting for her.

Serenai: So how have you been? What's new?
Chuchie: Well I am a senior now. I will be finished in the Spring.
That's great. So how did you guys meet? Serenai questioned as the waiter placed the bucket of wine and set up the glasses.
Chuchie: How did we meet baby?
Tony: I tapped her while she was sitting studying in the library listening to her Lauryn Hill CD. We talked for about thirty minutes and I told her I wanted to see her again.
Serenai: Awe, how romantic. College love. I never went to college.
Tony: So what do you do?
Serenai: I am writer. I write poetry and non-fiction.
Chuchie: Baby, this is Serenai. She wrote the book you got me for Valentine's Day this year, The Scarlet Letter.
Tony: No way. I read that book and loved it so I knew my lady would love it.
Serenai: Ha Ha Thanks for the support.
Tony: So you mean to tell me you know The Serenai and you were never going to tell me?
Serenai: You never asked.
Tony: I feel like a groupie right now. I am your biggest fan. If it doesn't work between me and Chuchie, you are next on the list.

They all began to laugh. The three of them drank wine and conversed until 12AM. They talked about politics, literature, college, music, poetry, and so much more. It seemed like they could talk about absolutely anything.

REFLECTIONS

Chuchie: Baby, we have to get up early in the morning. We have to go home.
Tony: Yea I guess you're right. We had so much fun with you tonight.
Serenai: I enjoyed your company very much. Maybe we can hang out again.

Maybe! Serenai replied. We will see you around. Tony said as he led Chuchie out the booth. Wait, here is my number. Serenai followed as she held her hand out to give the card to Chuchie. Tony grabbed the card and placed it in his pockets and him and Chuchie headed towards the door.

TONY'S PLAN

Tony: Why are you Serenai no longer friends and why have you never mentioned her?
Chuchie: There is a lot that I can't explain. I just don't want anything to do with her. Is that ok?
Tony: Sure I just don't understand why. She seems so nice.

Chuchie let the water from the shower hit her face and the steam flowed through her pores. She always felt so relaxed in the shower. This was her place of solitude and tonight she needed to be alone with her thoughts. Serenai wasn't a bad person at all. She was actually a very morally correct person. She just happened to be a lesbian. A lesbian that Chuchie had once fallen in love with.

After her relationship with Serenai, Chuchie had promised herself and God that she would never make that mistake again. She went outside of her faith to be with someone she could never have a future with. But now she knew that Serenai would try to ruin her relationship with Tony. She wondered if she should tell Tony before Serenai told him. She was so confused, but she knew she loved Tony so much and didn't want to lose him.

She turned off the water and grabbed her towel from the wall. She stepped out of the shower into her plush bedroom slippers. She then wrapped the towel around her. Her hair was hanging, she had just washed it with Tony's favorite shampoo. He had told her loved to smell Strawberry Melon in her hair. So now she kept a bottle only for special occasions. Tonight was a special occasion.

REFLECTIONS

Meanwhile, Tony was in the bedroom preparing for the moment. He was going to pop the question. He scattered rose petals over the bed. He had lit candles around window sills and he had light R&B playing. He stood outside of the bathroom door patiently awaiting her exit with two roses in hand. Each rose symbolized the years they had spent together. One had an engagement ring on it. When the doorknob finally began to turn, Tony's heart began to skip a beat.

Chuchie looked in amazement around the room at the bed, the candles, the lights, the radio, and then her eyes rested on Tony. He was wearing nothing but silky red boxer briefs and in his hand she noticed the roses. Tony then grabbed her hand and walked her to the bed and sat her down. Then he knelt down on his right knee. Chuchie's eyes began to water.

Tony began to speak. Ms. Chanel, I love you so much. You mean the world to me. I can't envision myself living without you. I am very proud to that you are mine, but I know that you are not really mine. Well at least not yet. I met you two years ago and since I have met you I have been a better man. You helped me see life as a blessing. You helped me realize that I shouldn't take life for granted and that I should always strive to be the best I can be. So I want to say to you Ms. Chanel Colita Jones, will you marry me? Chuchie was now crying and sobbing. She quickly began to wipe her face.

I have to tell you something first. I love you so much. But I don't want any secrets between us. I was feeling really exhausted for about a week straight and I wondered what was wrong with me. So I went to the doctor. As Chuchie continued, Tony's eyes began to water as if he knew what she were about to say. Baby, we are pregnant. Chuchie quickly confirmed. Tony quickly jumped up and grabbed her and began to kiss her. He began to tell her how much he loved her. But I have to tell you more. Chuchie said. What is it?

You know why I never mentioned Serenai?
No why?
She was just a phase of my past and I didn't want you judging me.
What you mean?
Me and her were in a relationship for a year and a half.
What?

I broke up with her because I knew that it was wrong and because I knew we could never have a family together.

Tony now had a confused look on his face. He didn't know what to say to this. He immediately began to think about his ex-girlfriend Mikayla. Mikayla was a white girl who was attending Southern Valley with him on an internship assignment from Soli Forum University. She was 5'2, 120 lbs, with blonde hair, huge titties, blue eyes, and pretty white skin. Tony and Kayla, as he called her, were dating for about five months. Then he asked her to take their relationship to the next level.

Let's have a threesome. He said as she sat down next to him. A threesome? Why and with who? She puzzled in shock. You and another female. It will be fun. He said. Another female? I've never been with another female. It would be weird. She said in disbelief still. I will be right there guiding you all the way. He said as he rubbed her back.

Kayla agreed to do it. Then on the day that it was supposed to happen, she dumped Tony for not just wanting to be with her. Tony had always wanted to try a threesome and he never got the opportunity to do so. Now the woman that he loved admitted that she had previously been in a relationship with a female. Tony began to quickly weigh the pros and cons of the situation and came up with a master plan. He would have a threesome with Serenai and Chuchie.

Tony: Woah. Thank God you weren't a man. I don't think I could have worked around that. The two began to laugh.
Chuchie: So you are okay with that?
Tony: Of course, it's in your past. You don't hold mine against me, so why should I hold yours against you?
Chuchie; Ha Ha I guess you are right. My answer is yes.

REFLECTIONS

Tony quickly grabbed Chuchie's towel and put it on the floor. He then picked her naked body up and scooted her up on the bed. He began to open her legs slowly. He placed her left foot in his mouth and sucked toe by toe as she moaned. Then he reached for her right foot and sucked toe by toe. Then he began to kiss her ankles and licking the soles of her feet. She moaned loudly and began to squirm. he began to kiss and lick up and down her thighs. He would leave drips of slob on each thigh and come back to them by licking them off very fast with his tongue. He reached for her vagina. He slowly began to finger her clit when he moved his face closer to her in a slithering motion. As he came to her vagina, he began to lick her clit and finger her pussy. He was now rock hard in his red silky boxer briefs. He quickly took them off and started to stroke his huge penis with his hand. Chuchie yearned for him to be inside her. She sat up and began to stroke it with her hand. Then she spit on it and began to suck it. Slowly sucking it in and out her mouth, gagging as he began to face fuck her. Then he whispered to her, I want to put it in you. She lay back on the bed. Then he entered her vagina. The two of them moaned in excitement.

Three weeks had passed since Tony had met Serenai. He wondered if his fantasy would ever become a reality. He noticed how beautiful she was. He also wondered what kind of relationship she had with Chuchie. He knew that in order to make it work, he would have to fix Chuchie's relationship with Serenai.

He now sat in the office in their home. The house belonged to Chuchie. When Sham had purchased it, he signed the property deeds in her name. The house had three bedrooms, two full bathrooms, and a den. The backyard was huge with a giant orange tree. When Sham was sentenced to life in prison, he wrote her a letter telling her she now owned the home. At first Chuchie thought of selling it, but then she decided she would keep it. When Tony and Chuchie began dating, Tony was living on campus. After a year of dating, Chuchie invited Tony to live with her. The den was turned into an office. Tony graduated a year before Chuchie. After college, he decided to start his own practice. The practice office was located in the den of their home.

He remembered Serenai giving him her card. He quickly began to search his desk for her card. He searched file cabinets. Then he searched through his stacks of papers on the far side of the office and there sat Serenai's card on top of Phino's casework. He immediately scanned the card for her number.

So what's up? How are you? Serenai asked. I'm fine. I'm only here because Tony wants me to work on our relationship, so don't get any ideas. Chanel iterated. Of course not! So let's talk. Serenai responded. Ok. Chanel said. Well you are still beautiful. Serenai said eying her. This isn't going to work. Chuchie replied as she began to stand up. I'm sorry, wait sit back down. Serenai reassured her.

The two sat at a table at the Reck's Cafe. It was a small Italian restaurant that the two would often visit while they were dating. The mood was very awkward for Chuchie she didn't know whether to leave or to stay. Serenai thought could her relationship with Chuchie really be over, could she really not lover her anymore.

I know you may hate me.
I don't hate you. I just don't want to be with you.
Why?
Because I'm in love with my man.
Really?
Yes, really.
So the thought of us never comes to mind?
No, you are the past and Tony is my future.
Ha ha. You're lying. You always were a horrible liar.
What...
You can't look me in the eyes and tell me, so you're lying.
You are crazy. I'm going home.
You want to make your boyfriend happy; you're going to have to sleep with me.
What?
It's obvious. What man in his right mind would let his girlfriend hang out with a lesbian?
He knows what you meant to me.
Exactly. We were lovers and he wants you to fuck me.
You are crazy, what the fuck is wrong with you?
So if he asked you…
Asked me what? There is nothing to ask.
Maybe I'm wrong; maybe he really wants you to have friends.
Of course you are wrong.

REFLECTIONS

Waiter! Chuchie yelled. She was furious. She could not believe what she was hearing. Serenai was trying to convince her that the man that she loved wanted her to be with Serenai. All she now wanted to do was go home to her Tony.

SHALIAH

Meanwhile, Tony walked into the convience store. He slowly walked pass the cashier to the snack aisle. He wondered how the night was going with Serenai and Chuchie. Are they making love to each other, is Chuchie being stubborn, or could the friendship actually be over are the thoughts that taunted him. He grabbed a pack of sugar cookies and a Toffee bar and headed towards the counter.

Tony? A sweet voice called from behind. What's up? How have you been? He asked as he realized who she was.

Shaliah was Tony's neighbor while growing up. Her and her family moved into the house next door to Tony's house when she was eight. Her mother was white and Guyanese and her father was an Indian of the Chattoo tribe. Her parents met after her mother finished high school and moved to Canada. Shaliah spent her first eight years in Toronto, Canada. Her father got a job as the chief financial officer at Wtyo Inc. in Hampton, Virginia, so the family relocated.

Shaliah and Tony were very close while growing up. Both were student athletes. Tony played football and ran track while Shaliah played basketball. Shaliah would go to all Tony's home games to support him. She was like the little sister that he never had.

REFLECTIONS

When Tony went off to college at Southern Valley in Dallas, Shaliah went to Prospect University in DC. The two both majored in psychology for their undergraduate studies but later pursued other studies along with psychology for their graduate studies. Shaliah played basketball and was the team captain her last two years of college. Along with her leadership, the prospect lady bulls won the NCWA championship two years in a row.

Shaliah graduated Magna Cum Laude from her university and was offered a position as an intern for a mental hospital in New York City. She accepted the offer and worked as an intern until the company offered her a full time position. After two months of working as a full time employee, Shaliah enrolled at Suthaca to get her masters in business administration and her PhD in Clinical Psychology. Twenty four months later, she crossed the stage as valedictorian.

In the ninth grade, Shaliah admitted to Tony that she was a lesbian. He always figured she was but never knew for sure until she told him. When she told him, he said I knew it. He helped her come out to her parents. She wrote a letter and let Tony read it.   After rewriting the letter twelve times, the thirteenth letter finally got his approval. When her parents read the letter, they immediately blamed Tony. The two would always hang out. Her parents assumed it was because Tony always had her around boys. Shaliah was so beautiful to Tony and he never understood why she was a lesbian when all the guys wanted her. He confessed to her parents saying that he didn't know she was gay but he had always assumed it and that he helped her write the letter. Shaliah was the first and closest lesbian he had ever known.

Shaliah you look great. Tony said as he hugged her. She was even more beautiful then she was growing up. 5'7, 145 lbs, long brown hair, green eyes, caramel skin, and a beautiful smile, she now stood. She wore blue jeans with the thighs ripped, some Jordan's, and a grey t-shirt. Tony remembered how she was always a tomboy as he noticed her attire.

So what brings you to Virginia Beach?
I was promoted. I am now the executive director at the Virginia Beach Mental Health Department. I just moved here about a month ago.
Wow that is so great. I have my own clinic myself.
Really, that is great. Where is Kayla?

CHARLIE KAAR

We are no longer together. I met someone new and you have to meet her and tell me if she is a keeper.
Ok, will do. We have to catch up.
Ok sure thing. Here is my card. Call me when you get the chance.
K, thanks. Talk to you soon.

      Beep. The horns blared from behind her as she sat texting at a green light. She was in a rush. She had stopped at the store to get some Advil, then she rushed home to take a quick shower and put on a business suit. She had been suffering from a massive headache all day. Now she rushed down Lamonte Street to get to the Reck's. She had a business meeting scheduled for 8:30 and it was now 8:25. She prayed that her client would patiently wait.

      As she turned down Marco Blvd, she realized she hadn't spoke with her mother since their heated conversation about gay marriage laws. Her mother accepted her as a lesbian, but she refused to accept gay marriage. Shaliah had dated a girl named Lisa a few years back. The relationship got really intense when Lisa asked her to marry her. Shaliah wanted to have children while Lisa believed that children would ruin their relationship. Shaliah told her mother that Lisa had proposed to her and her mother responded by not acknowledging Lisa anymore. She said she was a heathen and it would be best for Shaliah to break up with her. Shaliah dumped her after her mother went months without speaking to her for deciding to marry Lisa. But now that Shaliah was single, her mother still didn't accept the thought of gay marriage even though it was legal.

      She quickly parked the car and rushed to the front entrance. Reservations ma'am? The hostess puzzled as she walked in. No, I'm here for a meeting with Ms. Jacqueline Devo. She responded. Right this way. The hostess said before leading her to Ms. Devo.

      As the host showed her to the table, Shaliah's eyes circled the room. The Reck's was her favorite restaurant in town. She loved the art the restaurant displayed and the beautiful classic music they played. This was her favorite, so she would always have business meetings here. Then she looked across the room and she locked eyes with the most beautiful woman she had ever seen. The woman simply smiled at her and continued her conversation. Immediately she started to lust for the woman.

REFLECTIONS

Hi, Ms. Pallavi! It is a pleasure to meet you. The woman said as Shaliah approached the table. Hi, I'm sorry I'm late. Shaliah quickly responded as she began to seat herself.

Do you like sex?
Yes, I love it.
When is the last time you had sex?
Last night.
Do you practice safe sex?
No.
Why do you not practice safe sex?
Because I only sleep with women.
Are you a lesbian?
Yes I am.
How long have you known you were a lesbian?
Since I was twelve.
 So how many sex partners have you had?
I don't know maybe five or six.
Were all of them female?
No, one was a male.
A male?
Yes I have slept with a man before.
Really and what was that like for you?
It was horrible.
How was it horrible?

I was sixteen years old. It was the summer of 1982. He was very handsome. He sat next to me on the bus to go to Coney Island. We started talking and realized that we were both going to Coney Island, so we decided to hang out. Once we got there, we rode the rides, ate cotton candy, and walked the beach. Then as the sun began to set, we went under the pier and began to make out.

CHARLIE KAAR

I was wearing some black biker shorts and a red, white and blue t-shirt. He began to unbutton my pants. I asked what he was doing and he said he just wanted to see. I said ok. So he finally unbuttoned my pants and he began to slowly pull them down. I felt this warming sensation coming over my whole body. It was like eating a Surty Donut for the first time. I had no underwear on, so he began to touch me. Then he got on his knees and he started licking me. He pushed me back on the pole and put my right leg on his shoulder. He licked and licked and I moaned and moaned.

Then after five minutes, he stood up and slowly started kissing me. His kisses were so soft. He whispered to me, Can I put it in? I nodded my head and he began taking off his shorts. He then pulled out his penis. It was about ten inches and as thick as your arm. My God that thing was big. He slowly began to insert it in me. I cried ouch and he said it's ok. It will only hurt for a second. Then he pushed harder and harder as I cried in pain. Next thing you know, I was bleeding. He continued to fuck me. When I noticed the blood, I yelled stop to him but he kept going faster and faster. Then all of sudden, splash. He nutted in me. Blood and cum dripped down my legs. He pulled his pants up and walked off. I never saw him again.
So you were raped?
No, I wasn't raped. I was scarred.
So did this cause you to no longer to want to be with men?
Ha Ha. I asked myself that after my son was born. Will I ever sleep with a man again, will I tell him that I didn't know who his father was, or would I find a man to take care of my child.
So he got you pregnant your first time?
Yes he did?
And the child?
My son is in prison for attempted murder.
So does he know what happened to you?
Yes he does, that's why he is in prison.
So he tried to kill his father?
He tried to kill me.

Shaliah sat in awe as Ms. Devo explained her story. She just wished she had taken Ms. Devo to her house instead of The Reck's.

REFLECTIONS

About two years ago, my son Daniel met a girl named Kim. Kim was his first love. She was a college student at Soli Forum. The two were inseparable up until Kim met some girl.

What girl?

Stacy or something like that.

What does she have to do with anything?

Kim was sleeping with her.

What?

      One day, I went over to Daniel's house to clean for him. I would always clean at least once a month. He would leave a spare key under the doormat for me. So I began cleaning the house. The house was upstairs and downstairs. So I would start from the bottom and work my way to the top. So I was in the kitchen and I heard a loud thump. So I walked upstairs. As i was getting closer to his bedroom door, I heard what sounded like spanking. So I began to turn the knob of the door and there that girl was spanking Kim. Kim yelled and I quickly rushed back downstairs. She followed behind me and begged me to stop. We were just rehearsing for this upcoming play she told me. I knew she was lying but I pretended to believe her and left to go home.

      Three weeks passed and I decided I would talk to Kim about the situation. So I invited her over for lunch. She told me it was a mistake and that she really loved my son. He had popped the question to her a month before it happened and she had to experience it before they were married. She said she had been a little curious for years. Then we had a few drinks and she began acting like she was crazy. She took off all her clothes and then began to give me a lap dance.

Wait, you didn't? Shaliah cut off.

      Yes I did. She was giving me head when my son walked in on us. Kim told him it was all her fault, but he thought his lesbian mother was trying to steal the woman he loved. So he went to the kitchen and grabbed the turkey knife. He ran towards me and jabbed me right in the throat.

Wow!

I had to be rushed to the hospital. I was rushed into surgery. He punctured one of the major arteries in my neck.

So your son is in prison for attempted murder?

My son is in prison because he chose to be.

What do you mean?

CHARLIE KAAR

I agreed to drop the charges against him. He requested he be given the maximum sentence because if he was a free man he would kill me.
While he was growing up, did he know you were a lesbian?

Of course! When he turned eight years old I told him. I was dating Talia Reyes. She was quite a woman. When we first met, I told her my son didn't know about my lifestyle. She told me I would have to come out to him or he would hate me. So a little after his eighth birthday party, Talia came over. He really liked her. She was the first African American woman I had ever dated. She would always bring Daniel gifts and read him stories. For his eighth birthday she bought him a BB gun. She had worked on that day so she came a little after the party. We talked very briefly, and then it was time. I told him I was a lesbian and how he was really born. He was very shocked.
What was his response?
So is Talia my daddy?
What did you tell him?
His father was an evil man who had left a hole in my heart and Talia was there to fill that empty space.
So he accepted it?
Yes, he fully accepted it.
Talia and I were together up until Daniel was about fifteen when she decided she wasn't ready for commitment and left.
So how have you been handling this whole ordeal with your son?
He doesn't allow me to visit, respond to my calls or letters, and he threatens to kill me all the time.
Why do you think he handled the situation in such a way?
I think he really loved Kim and he felt threatened by her being with someone else.
I think your son has a problem with you being a lesbian.
Why do you say that?
Was Kim the first girl he ever introduced you to?
Yes but... He always brought over his friends.
There is no but. Friends are friends. Lovers are people with the potential to be soul mates. Your son never approved of your lifestyle but he knew he couldn't change your mind so he kept his distance.
He never acted as if though he didn't approve.
He wanted you to be happy but he wasn't happy with you. Did he ever try to fix you up?
All the time. He once tried to hook me up with his football coach.

Right. He wanted you to be with a man. He probably felt as if though if you found the right man you would change, but you didn't.

Wow! I never thought of it that way.

We don't pay attention to the things that are right in front of us. You wanted the best for him and he wanted the best for you. Which he believed to be a man, not a woman.

You are astonishing.

Why, thank you. This has been a lovely night. I have to get going, but I have a homework assignment for you.

What is it?

Write a letter to your son and ask him for forgiveness.

He doesn't respond.

This time I will be sending the letter myself. He will respond to me.

How do you know for sure?

I don't but I have to have a little faith.

Ok, good night Ms. Cook.

    As Shaliah left the table, her eyes searched the place for the woman she had noticed when she came in. She quickly spotted her now standing at the bar.

WHERE DID I GO WRONG?

Trinity State was to host a debate in three days. Shaliah was now working on her campaign for council woman. Her major opponents were Ron Slanslow, a Jewish Republican, and Harry Toledo, a Christian democrat. With the move to Virginia Beach, Shaliah was offered an internship offer with Speak Up or Die campaign. It was an equal opportunity campaign that supported gay marriage, abortion, marijuana legalization, less taxes, free education, free health care, and a less heinous criminal justice system. While campaigning, Shaliah worked hard. She worked overtime to push for the causes that she believed in. Then when the next election was around the corner, the party nominated her as a candidate for the election. She accepted their offer and began her campaign.

Shaliah wasn't your typical running mate. She didn't have her campaigners doing all the work; she handled most of it herself. She wrote many proposals and also wrote all of her own speeches. She toured the district she was running for weekly. She held many community events and even went as far as becoming a mentor at one of the schools. She was actually a hard worker for the community. She believed the only way to help the community was by actually being involved in the community.

REFLECTIONS

She was an African American at heart but was viewed by the world as a white girl. While growing up, she dealt with many issues regarding her skin color and her sexuality. After many years of dealing with all the turmoil, she now knew that she was who she was and no matter how harsh society's views of her were, she wasn't changing. She believed that equality meant a person should not be discriminated against because of their sexuality, religion, race, etc.

Shaliah sat patiently as she heard cheers of the crowd. She wondered if being here tonight would affect her career. Then suddenly the crowd got silent as a woman walked onto stage. Shaliah quickly turned to see what was going on. She sat at a bar on the far side of the lounge. The place was packed for this month's poetry reciting. She wasn't really into poetry but she always loved coming to The Flask.

As she turned she noticed the crowd was still silent. Then she spotted the reason why. A woman in all black stood on the stage silently in all black with a rose in her hand. She just stood there holding rose as tears rolled down her cheeks. Shaliah wondered what she had missed. When she entered the lounge, she sat at the bar and had a few drinks as she pondered about her campaign.

WHERE DID I GO WRONG
WAS I LOST IN MYSELF
WAS I HURTING DEEP INSIDE AND NEVER GOT
HELP
WAS MY REALITY TRULY HELL
WAS MY PAIN COVERED UP BY LOVE AND
DECEIT
OR WAS I NAÏVE
WAS I TOO BLIND TO SEE
I WAS SO IN LOVE WITH ME
THEN CAME HE
HE WAS ALL I COULD EVER NEED
THE MAN I NEVER KNEW ANYONE COULD BE
I CRIED AND CRIED WHEN THE DOCTORS TOLD
ME
I HAD HIV
NOW I WONDERED HOW
I HAD ONLY BEEN WITH ONE MAN SO HOW
HE WAS SO PERFECT SO WHAT WAS I TO DO NOW
SO I ASKED WHAT HE HAD DONE BEFORE HE
MET ME
HE TOLD ME HE LIVED ON THE STREETS
AND THAT'S WHEN I REALIZED MY MAN WAS
LIVING SECRETLY
NOW WITH ONLY THREE MONTHS TO LIVE I
WEAR ALL BLACK AND THIS ROSE
NOT BECAUSE IM DEPRESSED OR SAD BUT SO
THAT EVERYONE CAN KNOW
I WILL NEVER HIDE SUCH A PROBLEM AS THIS
JUST FOR THE SAKE OF MY NOSE
MY HUSBAND CONTRACTED HIV FROM CASUAL
SEX WITH MEN AND SHOOTING
UP DOPE
SO NOW THAT ALL IS DONE
I WISH MY LIFE COULD BE LONG
BUT I REALIZE WHERE I DID GO WRONG

REFLECTIONS

The audience began to snap as the woman walked off stage. Many patted her as walked through the crowd. It was like a funeral had just ended and no one knew whether or not to smile or cry. Shaliah sat at the bar now with tears in her eyes. She wondered why she felt so sad for the woman. Maybe it was because a man had cursed her or maybe it was because she thought the woman was so beautiful.

A man then came on stage following her reciting. Give it up for the beautiful Sheyana Ban. It was such a pleasure to have her here back where she got her start in poetry many years ago. We all want you to know we still love you and you will go down in history as the woman who never gave up. So thank you for that.

Shaliah knew the name sounded familiar. She quickly began to think I know her. Then she remembered. Sheyana was Shaliah's first crush in high school. She was the captain of the cheerleading squad and graduated from high school as valedictorian. Shaliah met her in an English Literature class. The two were put together in group project. They had to create a five minute documentary about different genres of poetry.

Sheyana was an exceptional poet. She knew everything there was too know about poetry, while Shaliah didn't. So to complete the documentary, Sheyana gave a book called A Lover's quarrel and told her to read it and write a summary of the book. Shaliah read the book overnight and loved it. She had never read such a book. The book made her feel at ease with her sexuality. When Sheyana and Shaliah discussed it, she told her it made her accept herself more. Sheyana told her she knew it would.

The group made a documentary that only featured the two of them. It was called A Lover's Quarrel. The two were set to be married to the same man. Sheyana's character married the man in a small city and Shaliah's character married him in another country. Sheyana's character was now a mother when she met a young woman. She falls in love with the woman. The woman is Shaliah's character. After over two years of a secret affair between the two, Shaliah's character confessed to Sheyana's character that she was married. Sheyana confessed as well. Then the two realized their husband was the same man. So the two confronted him about the situation and he revealed to them that he was married to four other women.

It showcased poetry in many different dimensions. The topic of the documentary was how poetry can be used to express feelings. Poetry in *A Lover's Quarrel* was used to show cultural differences, what's socially and politically acceptable, and how to deal with tough situations.

As Sheyana walked through the crowd with her head down in sorrow, Shaliah wondered if she should go speak. So she quickly rose from her seat and began to move towards her. She suddenly appeared right before her. The woman quickly stopped as if though he had just seen a ghost. Hi Sheyana! What have you been up to? Shaliah quickly questioned. Still with a perplexed look on her face, she responded, what are you doing here? Excuse me? Why are you here tonight? I just came to check out the scene. I didn't expect to see you here, but since you are I decided I would speak. Being here will ruin your career. Don't you know that you are in a gay club? Yes I do, Shaliah laughed.

Sheyana was so confused. She didn't understand why someone would risk their career in such a manner. How about we go grab some coffee and catch up? Sheyana quickly reassured. She led Shaliah to the exit and told her to meet her at the Waffle House on Fifth Street. The two split up and headed for Waffle house.

Sheyana: This is a much safer place for us to talk.

Shaliah: I don't understand what you mean.

Sheyana: I mean you are crazy for even thinking about such a thing.

Shaliah: So I have to pretend not to be myself for the sake of my campaign.

Sheyana: Exactly, no one will accept you for being a lesbian. Politics don't work in such a manner.

Shaliah: I really don't care. If it's meant to be it shall be.

Sheyana: Right. How are you my love?

Shaliah: I'm well. As you already know, I'm running for a seat in council.

Sheyana: That will be good for you. I always loved that about you.

Shaliah: What is that?

Sheyana: You never give up on the things you believe in. So where is the lucky lady?

Shaliah: There is no one. I'm all by myself.

Sheyana: Really?

Shaliah: Yea. It really sucks because I thought she was the one.

Sheyana: Wow, I'm sorry to hear that. Maybe it wasn't the right timing.

Shaliah: Yea I guess not. I'm sorry for your loss.

Sheyana: I have something to tell you, but I would rather show you.

Shaliah: Ok, what is it.

Sheyana: Let's meet up on Wednesday at the Freemont hotel. Promise not to judge me.

Shaliah: Of course not. You were my first friend.

The two shared coffee and conversed for a few more hours, and then suddenly there she was again. The beautiful woman that she had saw earlier while dinning with her client was now about ten feet away from her sitting in a booth.

Shaliah, are you okay? Sheyana questioned as Shaliah gazed behind her. Yea I just. Nothing! Never mind! Shaliah reassured. Sheyana turned slowly to see what had grabbed Shaliah's attention. Two very beautiful women sat two booths behind them.

I haven't been in here in years. Chuchie said as she looked around. Really I still come and enjoy waffles every now and then. Serenai confirmed. Cool. Chuchie acknowledged. I'm really happy for you. I hope that he is as great as you say he is. Serenai stated. He is. He is more perfect than you. Chuchie reassured. Well he must be good. So how many months are you? Serenai questioned. I'm two months in and really excited. Chuchie responded.

Chuchie looked up from the table and looked around the establishment. It was almost three in the morning and slow jams played from the juke box. Chuchie noticed that there were only three other people in the place. There was an old white man at the far side. There were two women seated two booths away from them. The woman facing towards Chuchie locked her eyes in on her.

As Chuchie noticed the woman gazing at her, she winked at her as Serenai walked to the register to pay for dinner. The woman acknowledged Chuchie signaling her head towards the bathroom as if though she was telling her to meet her in there. So Chuchie told Serenai she would meet her outside as she walked towards the restroom.

CHARLIE KAAR

What was that? Sheyana questioned. Nothing. Shaliah said as she began to stand up. I guess this is good night my love. Sheyana replied as she began to stand. Yes, I will see you Wednesday. This was my treat. I enjoyed your company. Good night. Shaliah said as she walked towards the restroom.

As Chuchie entered the restroom she didn't know what to expect. She wondered what the woman knew about her or her dearest Tony. She paced back and forth. Shaliah didn't know whether to just walk up to the woman and say she was interested or pretend not to want to her for the sake of her career. She slowly pushed open the restroom door.

She walked in slowly and began to lean on a wall and watch Chuchie pace back and forth. Chuchie hadn't noticed that the woman had walked in. She continued to pace until she felt like someone was watching her. She stood silent between the sinks and the stalls and slowly began to turn around.

How long have you been there? Chuchie questioned. Not long. What are you up to? Shaliah responded. Nothing much! My name is Chanel. Chuchie said reaching out her hand to her. I'm Shaliah. Shaliah said as she shook her hand. That name sounds so familiar. Who are you? Chuchie questioned. I just told you who I was. Shaliah said jokingly. What do you want with me? Chuchie puzzled. I wanted to know your name. Shaliah said as she stared into Chuchie's eyes. Why? Chuchie wondered. Because you are beautiful! Shaliah said as she gazed at the woman who stood before her.

I'm engaged to be married. Chuchie iterated as she lifted her hand. Right! Shaliah said in disbelief. No I really am. Chuchie reiterated. So why did you wink at me? Shaliah questioned. I don't know, I was just…. Chuchie started. You were just what? She cut her off. I never would have thought this was the reason you wanted to meet me in here. Chuchie said as she began to feel a little dizzy.

What else would it have been for? You didn't think I needed a pad did you? Shaliah joked. You're an asshole. Chuchie responded as she turned to face the woman. Why am I an asshole? Shaliah puzzled. Because you think this is funny. Chuchie raged. No, I think you are funny. Shaliah said as she stepped closer to Chuchie. I'm this close to…. Chuchie began. Yea I see. Shaliah cut her off.

REFLECTIONS

Shaliah began to caress Chuchie's arm. She slowly began to move closer to her. Her heart began to beat rapidly. She could hear Chuchie's beat as well. I just want to hold you. Do I have permission? Shaliah questioned as she began to wrap her arms around Chuchie's waist.

Chuchie longed for a woman's touch. She wanted to say no but her body wouldn't allow her to. The two slowly embraced one another as Shaliah began to kiss Chuchie's neck. Up, down, and from right to left she flicked her tongue across Chuchie's sensitive skin. As she passionately licked her neck, she began to massage her breasts. Shaliah then moved from her neck to deep tongue kisses with her. She moved her tongue in and out of Chuchie's mouth as she massaged her breast. Chuchie moaned in ecstasy.

Shaliah slowly guided Chuchie to the wall. Now Chuchie stood with her back to the wall. Chuchie had on a small black dress. Shaliah noticed the dress was very small and began to slowly lift the dress. Chuchie was wearing a brown panties and bra set. It made her skin radiate in the light. Shaliah had now pushed the dress over Chuchie's head and pulled it off. Chuchie stood with nothing but heels and lingerie on. Shaliah slowly began to pull Chuchie's panties off leg by leg as the two stared into each other's eyes. Shaliah began to lick the inside of Chuchie's thighs. As she got closer and closer to Chuchie's womanhood, Chuchie's breathing became heavier and heavier.

Serenai sat patiently awaiting Chuchie in her car. She remembered how Chuchie would always take forever in the restroom. She reached into her ash tray and grabbed the other half of the blunt she had been smoking earlier and quickly lit it. After Serenai and Kim ended their relationship, Serenai started smoking. She quit after starting a relationship with Chuchie. She started again after Chuchie and her ended it. As she smoked the blunt she wondered what was taking Chuchie so long. She began thinking of the worst. She put out the blunt, exited the car, and locked it. She walked towards the front of the establishment and peeped through the window. She remembered Chuchie telling her she would catch up, but that was an hour ago.

No, wait, stop, Chuchie quickly asserted. What's wrong? Shaliah asked as she gazed up at Chuchie. I haven't been with a woman in a long time. I don't even know you. This isn't how I wanted this to happen. Chuchie replied slowing down her breathing. Yea, you are right. Here's my card. Call me when you are ready. Shaliah continued as she reached into her pocket to give her the card. Chuchie took the card and place it in her bra; leaned down to grab her dress and panties, slowly put them back on, and exited out of the restroom.

Then Chuchie walked out of the restroom. She looked as if though she had just woke up. Serenai quickly walked to the door and held it open as Chuchie walked out. Are you ok? Serenai questioned as they walked towards Chuchie's car. I'm fine. I just had a little scare that's all. Chuchie said reluctantly. Do you want me to take you to the hospital? Serenai asked with concern. No I'm fine Chuchie reassured as they approached her car. She kissed Serenai on the cheek and told her she would call her when she got home. Then she got into her car and began to drive away when she spotted Shaliah walking out of the door. She watched her cross the street as Serenai walked back to her car.

Serenai went the opposite way, so Chuchie decided she would go and speak to Shaliah. Hi stranger she said as she pulled up alongside the woman. I thought I would never see you again she said as she rolled down her window. Maybe you will, maybe you won't. Chuchie joked. We will see. Shaliah responded. Farewell, Ms. Shaliah. Chuchie replied as she drove off.

When she entered the house she hoped that Tony was fast asleep so she wouldn't have to explain her night. She tip toed to the kitchen. She cut on the lights in the kitchen and slowly began to undress. She was wet and she knew that Tony would know that she was unfaithful if she were to lie next to him already wet. As she finished undressing, she turned out the kitchen lights, grabbed her clothes, and rushed to the downstairs bathroom. She turned on the light and then turned the hot water on in the shower. As the room began to fog up, she thought about her night. Then she remembered the card. She looked down at her clothes that sat below her on the floor. The card lay right in the left cup of her bra. She grabbed the card and glanced at it. It read in bold, black letters:

REFLECTIONS

Dr. Shaliah Pallavi
Executive Director
Virginia Beach Mental Health Department
(757)312-2025 ext. 112
(347)892-9141

Chuchie tried to remember where she had heard the name before. It just would not register in her head. After almost giving herself a migraine from thinking too much, Chuchie entered the shower. The bathroom was now very steamy. Chuchie loved this feeling. She washed her body as if she was trying to wash off her skin tonight. She knew Tony would know that she was with someone else if she didn't wash away the woman's sweet kisses.

After her shower, Chuchie decided she would finally get some rest. She took her clothes to the laundry room, then began up the stairs for bed. As she entered the room, she noticed Tony wasn't in the bed. The bed was neatly made. She now looked puzzled and wondered where her man was.

MR. GLOWNEIC

Tony slowly cruised the streets at five in the morning. Then he came to a stop on Biscayne Blvd in front of an old cherry oak home. The house sat at the end of the street alone. It was the only wooden house on the block. Tony knew that he would be in here for long. So he quickly reached into the glove compartment and grabbed his bible. He turned it to Psalms 56 and began to read. After he finished reading, he said a quick prayer.

As he finished his prayer, he noticed the front porch light come on. He placed the bible back into the glove compartment. Then he took the keys out the ignition, got out of the car, locked the door, and placed the keys into his pocket. He proceeded towards the front porch. He knew that the door would already be open once he got onto the porch. As he reached to open the door, an old man stood in the door in nothing but his underwear.

REFLECTIONS

Mr. Glowneic, please go inside. Tony said as he showed the man into the house. They took my money and gave it to them damn bunnies. Now I can't buy me nothing to eat. The man said as he walked back into the house. He responded. Mr. Glowneic, I told you that there is no one. I gave you my cell to call when you had an emergency. Tony reiterated. So where is my money and my food? He questioned. Tony walked towards the kitchen. He turned on the lights in the kitchen. He walked to where the refrigerator was and began to point saying, Mr. Glowneic all of your food is in here or in one of those cabinets. After completing his sentence he opened the refrigerator, and just as he suspected there was plenty of food.

Mr. Larry Glowneic was Tony's first client when he opened his practice. He was a marine's veteran. He had served in the service for twenty five years. After ten years, he met a woman by the name of Tracy Lovine in Germany. Tracy was working at the station as a nurse practitioner. Larry was shot in the arm and he needed immediate medical attention. After intensive surgery was performed on him, he was left in a hospital rehabilitation center. Nurse Lovine was his nurse. Each day she would clean his wound and sing to him. As he got better, he began to walk the halls of the hospital. The two of them began to take walks together holding hands.

Then one day he received orders telling him to report for departure. He didn't want to lose Tracy because he had falling in love with her. So the two rushed to get married and when it was time for departure, she returned to the US with him. The two found a home in Virginia Beach where they decided to start a family. After four years of being home and after the birth of his first daughter, Rebecca, Larry was deployed to Germany again. He served for five years and was allowed to return home to his family. This time while at home, he and Tracy had a son. They named him Larry Jr. Then five years later, they had their last child Elizabeth. On Elizabeth's second birthday, he was summoned for deployment to Germany again. This time while serving he was shot in the head. The bullet went through his skull and grazed his brain leaving him mentally unstable for the rest of his life.

CHARLIE KAAR

He was sent home to recover. His wife cared for him, the children, and took care of the house until she died on Elizabeth's eighteenth birthday. Many believed she lived long enough to make sure Elizabeth was old enough to take care of herself. Her children believed she died from a broken heart because their father had forgotten who they were. After the passing of their mother, Rebecca had her father place in a senior citizens home. After six years of turmoil, Rebecca decided it would be best for her father to live the rest of his days at home.

After a year of staying at home with her father, she decided she couldn't do it. She hired Tony Alexander. He was a recently certified psychologist and had opened his own practice. After many brain tests, psychiatric treatments, and analytical assumptions, he told her that her father suffered from Alzheimer's disease. He needed love, support, and understanding.

From then on, Tony was Mr. Glowneic's shrink. Mr. Glowneic accepted Tony as he was his own son. He called him for everything. Whether it was to find his socks, to go to the bathroom, to read a book, or even to watch TV, he called Tony. Rebecca paid all of Mr. Glowneic's bills and always made sure he had food to eat and clothes to wear. Tony's job was to be the love and support that Mr. Glowneic needed.

If you are hungry, fix yourself something to eat from here. Tony demanded as he pointed at the refrigerator. Ok. He replied as he turned and began to walk away. Tony knew that Mr. Glowneic was going to sit in his favorite chair and talk for another hour or so, so he followed behind him. As Mr. Glowneic got comfortable in his chair, Tony sat on the sofa directly across from him.

Now son, when are you going to get married and start a family? Mr. Glowneic questioned Tony. Tony was very shocked. He and Mr. Glowneic had never talked about his love life. He didn't know what to say. Did you hear me boy? Mr. Glowneic questioned. Yes sir. I… You what boy? He quickly asked. Sorry I just never thought you cared to know. What's her name? Chanel. Tony replied. Is she beautiful? Yes she is both inside and out. Tony blushed.

REFLECTIONS

So you love her? Larry questioned. Yea, she is the one. When is your Pa going to meet the girl? Larry questioned. Very soon, sir! I asked her to marry me. Tony replied. What? Larry questioned. Yea, I asked her to marry me. Tony replied. Is she pregnant? Larry questioned. Yea, but I didn't know until after I asked her. Tony replied. So she kept it from you? Larry questioned. Yea but it was because she had just found out. Tony replied. Bring her by here tomorrow so I can meet her, you understand me boy? No son of mine is going to be marrying any old woman. He demanded. Yes sir. I should get going. Ok don't forget now boy. Tony replied.

Today I want to introduce you to someone. Tony said as he placed Chuchie down on the counter. Ok. She replied as she leaned into Tony's chest. He is going to love you just as much as I do. He said as he nibbled on her hair. Who is it? She questioned as she lifted her face from his chest. Mr. Glowneic, one of my clients. He answered. You mean the old man who thinks he's your father? Chuchie asked. Yea! He answered. Ok let's make it happen. She joked as she hopped from the counter.

As they pulled up to the house, Chuchie's heart began to beat. She knew that Mr. Glowneic held a very dear place in Tony's heart. She really wanted to impress him. All the time Tony talked about Mr. Glowneic, she often found herself being jealous of the relationship the two of them had. She was now finally going to get to meet there other half of Tony's heart and it both excited her and scared her.

Tony walked around to open Chuchie's door. He reached out for her hand as she stepped out the car. She looked at the house and wondered why it was the only house at the end of the street. The two started walking towards the door as Tony closed her door. When they reached the door, Tony reached for his keys and began to unlock the door. When he entered the house, it smelled like someone had been cooking.

CHARLIE KAAR

A young man sat in Mr. Glowneic's favorite chair. He had pale skin, blue eyes, and long, curly, blonde hair. He quickly rose to his feet to greet Tony. You must be tired he said as he reached out his hand to Tony. Larry? I thought you... Tony began to question. This must be the lucky lady. Mr. Glowneic finished as he entered the room along with Rebecca and another younger woman. Rebecca had a smile as wide as the ocean on her face. Rebecca, it is good to see you. Tony said as he rushed to hug her. The two embraced each as if though they hadn't seen each other in years. Left looking lost and confused, Chuchie stood silently. Then Tony remembered, this is my fiancé Chanel. Everyone in the room gazed at her in astonishment.

I am Elizabeth, the youngest of my father's children next to Tony that is. She joked as she embraced Chuchie. The woman had radiant skin, long blonde hair, green eyes, and the body of a goddess. She was flawless. What's going on? Chuchie questioned. My father is having a celebration for his youngest son. But he's not. Chuchie uttered. We have openly accepted Tony into our family. My father loves him. She said as she gazed at him as if she would eat him alive.

I am Larry Jr., the young man interrupted. Me and your fiancé played football together at Southern Valley. He was my right hand man you know. He continued. I think that any woman takes this man out of the dog pound has to be sweet.

Where is Sherry and the kids Larry? Tony puzzled. They're visiting her mom for a few days. She just got out of the hospital. He answered. You guys have been together so long man. Tony finished. Yea and she is pregnant again. Larry confirmed. What? Tony quizzed. Yea, it's baby number three and I think we will be the last one. Larry finished.

Tony I want to say congratulations. Thank you for always being a great man to me and the world around you. And Chanel I hope for you the best with your future endeavors with my son and my grandson. Mr. Glowneic said as they all gathered around the table.

ELIZABETH

Elizabeth looked appalled. She couldn't believe what she was hearing. Could everything she once had with Tony really be finished? Was she to forget the love that Tony and she had shared, to let go of the past, and just pretend like she was ok with this announcement? She walked into the kitchen and grabbed the bottle of whiskey from the freezer and began to drink from it. After a quarter of the bottle was finished, she returned to the table where everyone was now enjoying the meal that she and Rebecca had made.

Tony and Elizabeth had met at homecoming at Southern Valley. Elizabeth had never been to college. She decided to pursue her career as a model. She had worked with Armani, Chanel, Tommy Hilfiger, Ralph Lauren, and Dolce & Gabana before she was twenty six years old. She was visiting the campus for her brother's first national television broadcast. She promised she would be there to support him. She brought along a few of her model friends to make her brother look good on national television.

CHARLIE KAAR

It was the Gold Bowl and her brother was the quarterback. It was his final year in college and he was looking to be drafted to the NFL. So Elizabeth really wanted to support him. She arrived on campus the previous Sunday before the game. Her and her model friends were staying at one of the girls' sorority house. Tony was invited to come to a mixer at the house. He brought along Larry, Coolie, and Trenard. The three of them were looking to find a girl to fornicate with, while Tony was still suffering from a broken heart.

He told the guys that Kim had broken up with him. But he didn't tell them why. He knew they would clown him for being so stupid. So he just came to the party because the guys couldn't get in without him. But he didn't want to find anyone.

Come on bruh. It was her lost. Trenard said as he looked at Tony moping. Why don't you at least try to bag a hunny to help you release? Coolie questioned as he walked towards the guys. Larry was already on the other side of the house talking to a group of girls. Tony ignored them and walked to the front of the house. He walked out the door. It was a nice breeze flowing on that night. Dallas, Texas was always cool in the night. He sat on the swing that slowly moved with the breeze.

What are you talking about? The first girl said. You can have any guy you want and you choose to sit around and wait for that douchebag Turk. The second girl finished. I love him. He is everything to me. Elizabeth responded. It's like we are meant to be, she continued.

The girls strolled passed the twilight fountains as they continued their conversation. One of my sorority sisters says that he like has a girlfriend at every school in Dallas. Like that's totally such a player move. The second girl continued. I'm not saying that black guys are better than white guys; but like my boyfriend treats me like a queen. The first girl stated.   Aren't you like dating that one guy who raps? The second girl questioned. Yea and it's totally true. They like have the biggest penises I have ever seen. The three of them laughed.

They finally approached Merill Hall. They had been viewing the campus for the past hour or so and it was now nine o clock. Are you sure you don't want to hang out tonight? The first girl questioned. I'm positive. Elizabeth reassured them as she hugged each one of them good night. Alright, call us when you get back to the house. The second girl yelled as the two of them waved Elizabeth off.

REFLECTIONS

It took her fifteen minutes to reach the sorority house. She thanked God she had never gone to college. She thought how she would never want to walk all over that or any other campus that was as huge. But she wondered what it was like to date a college student. She had heard so many great stories from her friends who went to college. Some of them dated frat guys, football players, basketball players, rappers, and male models. She longed for the intelligence of a college guy.

As she approached the porch, she noticed a guy sitting in the swing with his head down. She thought I should be a Good Samaritan and see what is wrong. She approached the swing and sat down. She placed her hand on his back and began to caress it. He slowly lifted his head. The two locked eyes as she rubbed his back. My name is Elizabeth. I just wanted to make sure you were ok. She told him. A smile came across his face as bright as the sun. I'm fine; I'm just relaxing. He responded as he stood from the swing. She followed standing as well. Ok, cool. So what's your name? She questioned. My name is Tony. He said as he reached out his hand for her to shake it. She shook his hand as they gazed in each other's eyes.

So what's your major? She puzzled. I'm a psych major. He replied. Cool. What about you? I'm not a student. I'm here to cheer on my brother for his last homecoming game. That's sweet of you. I'm on the team too. He replied. Yea? What position do you play? She puzzled. Right now, I'm a running back. But next season I'll be the quarterback for the team. He replied. That's nice. So do you want to go inside and enjoy the party? She puzzled. No, not really. I only came because my boys thought I should. He replied.

What your girlfriend said you couldn't come or something? She puzzled. No I just don't really care for parties and I don't have a girl. He replied as he eyed her. Why doesn't a guy like you have a girl? You're not gay are you? She puzzled. Hell no. I love pussy. He confirmed. Sorry I was just asking. She puzzled. Yea, are you lesbian? He asked. No, I don't even look like a lesbo. She responded. What exactly do they look like? He questioned. Anyone other than me! She reiterated. Right, so where is your boyfriend? Tony questioned. He is in New York City on a business trip. She answered. Yea, that's pretty cool I guess. He responded.

CHARLIE KAAR

It was now like two in the morning. Tony and Elizabeth had been walking and talking all over campus. I guess I should walk you back to the house now. I have curfew at three. If I'm not in my room for check in, I might get benched for homecoming. I understand. Tony stated. There is always tomorrow. She replied. Tony walked her back to house and stopped at the steps. So I'll see you around? Tony questioned as they stood outside of the sorority house. Yea, sure thing superstar! She said as she stared into his eyes as if she wanted to kiss him. Well good night lovely. He responded as she walked into the front door.

The next day came and all Elizabeth could think about was Tony. He was so sweet and charismatic with her. The way that he spoke about his love for football and the love he had for his family enticed her. The two had spent hours walking and talking and not once did he mention sex to her. She thought he was such a gentleman. She hoped that she would run into him today.

It was four o' clock and Elizabeth had decided to get something to eat from The Blanks. The Blanks was the student union building on campus. It housed three game rooms, two fitness areas, five different dining locations, a movie theater, a bowling alley, a swimming pool, and four computer labs. She decided she was in the mood for a burger and fries, so she went to Tek's. It was a small burger stop on campus with great burgers and shakes.

As she stood in line, she wondered what Turk was doing. So she grabbed her cell phone out her Armani purse and called him. Hey this is Turk. Sorry I'm not available but if you leave your name, your number, and a brief message, I might call you back. The voicemail played after two rings. She hung the phone up as the line started to get smaller.

So I banged her after her friend gave me head. Then she gave her friend some head. Then I fucked her sister. It was a nice night. Larry preached as the guys walked off the field. Are you serious? Coolie questioned. Nah, he lying! There is no way that this no game having ass honky had sex with three girls last night. Trenard joked. Why you such a hater? White boy can't jump, but he sure can score. Tony acknowledged as he shook Larry's hand. Yea, whatever I don't believe it. Trenard hated. You don't have to. Just know I banged your sorority sister. Larry joked.

REFLECTIONS

The guys had just finished up practice. There routine had become to always be the last guys off the field after practice. Man, you fucked Sherry? Coolie questioned as he placed he cleats in his locker. Yea, why? Awe man you're the man. Coolie applauded as he shook Larry's hand. She been shallow with the pussy since day one. He affirmed. Yea man! I fucked Gina and tried to fuck her but she always played the I'm too good for you shit. Trenard confirmed. What? She is the biggest freak I ever met in my life. She sucked my dick the first night we hung out. By the next weekend, in between her classes we were fucking in the backseat of her Benz. Larry preached. Damn. Alright, you the man! Trenard cheered. I thought Tony was the biggest player but you take the cake. Coolie shouted. Come on, y'all know these girls love the eyes. Tony quickly added. I have the green and he has the ocean. Tony joked as he looked at Larry. Yea I have to get me some contacts. So these bitches can be all on my dick. Trenard suggested. The guys all laughed as they walked out of the locker room.

So lunch on the ocean right? Trenard joked as the guys approached The Blanks. Yea I guess. He answered. But nothing too fancy. All white people ain't rich. He joked. The guys all loved Tek's, so they quickly walked over to the line. Yo, there she go right there. Trenard whispered as Sherry walked towards them. Hi guys! She said as she walked up to them with Gina.

Sherry was a member of Kappa Zeta Delta, the sister sorority of the Sigma Alpha Psi fraternity. Gina was also a member. Sherry was about 5'4, 145 lbs, with pretty chocolate skin, and long, black hair. She had nice hips and a nice shaped butt. She was thick but not too thick. Her eyes were light brown and gleamed when the light hit her face. Gina was also a chocolate complexioned woman with acne all over her face. She was about 5'1, 180 lbs, and had natural short hair. She had huge tits and a moderate butt.

Larry was madly in love with Sherry but couldn't admit it for the sake of his manhood. He had also lied about his relationship with her. The two had never had sex together or even talked about sex. She was his best friend and he told her everything besides the fact that he loved her. He had always been there for her. After each horrible break up, he was there by her side. She always told him how much he meant to her, but Larry longed for her to be his love.

CHARLIE KAAR

Hi Larry! Sherry gleamed. Hey what's up? Larry responded. Are you coming tonight, you promised you would? Sherry puzzled. Yea I'll be there. But is it ok if the fellas come? Larry responded. Of course! Trenard is family and I don't see why Tony and Coolie can't come. She said as she glanced over at them. Yea we should all enjoy the night she continued as she stared at Tony. Larry noticed the look she gave Tony and immediately felt horrible. Tony, will you come hang out with us tonight? Gina questioned as she gazed at Tony. Yea sure I'll see what's up. He shrugged. The ladies said there farewells and left the guys standing in line.

A piece of Larry was hurting inside. He didn't know what to do about his feelings for Sherry. He had waited so long to tell her how he really felt that she was starting to take interest in Tony. He knew that if Sherry and Tony were ever left alone in the same room, his chances of ever being with her were over. He fantasized of a life where he and Sherry were married, had three sons, lived in a huge house, and he played for the NFL. She was his dream woman. She reminded him of his mother, so loving and smart.

Bruh, wake up. Tony said as he shook Larry. Larry quickly came back to reality. I'm good. I think I just need to sit down for a minute. He replied as he reached into his wallet and handed Tony his credit card. Alright, we can't have you getting sick before the game. Tony worried. Yea I know. I'll be over there sitting. Just get me a strawberry shake, a cheeseburger, and some loaded fries. He said as he walked towards a table at the other end of the room.

The others also told Tony what they wanted and followed behind Larry. Tony now stood in line alone. He began to think of Kim. He wondered if his choice to ask her to have a threesome with him had really ruined his relationship or was it something more. He was perfect to her. He had introduced her to his family and they loved her just as much as he did. He thought their relationship was perfect and she would do anything for him.

The line was so long. People started getting out of line and going to Freta's. After so many people had got out of line, Tony was finally closer to the front. He was lost in his thoughts when he noticed a huge gap in the line. He rushed closer to the counter where he now stood fourth in line. As he looked he noticed a woman in front of him. She stood on her hind legs and had a nice butt. Tony gazed at her. He moved closer to get a closer look at her. When he realized that it was Elizabeth, he wrapped his arms around her.

REFLECTIONS

Hey shortie! He whispered in her ear. She quickly pulled away and turned to see who was whispering in her ear. Oh my god, I thought I was going to have to mace someone. She joked. The two laughed. How are you today? He questioned as he stopped laughing. I'm fine, just trying to get a burger. I've been standing in this line for thirty minutes. She whined. Yea, it's Tek's. The slowest service, but the best food. So what are you doing later? She questioned him as the line began to move again. I'm going to the Kappa Zeta Delta party. He replied. What is that? She puzzled.

It's this sorority on the other side of campus. He responded. Oh. I've never heard of them. She said. Yea it's a black sorority. He affirmed. Maybe you should go to experience a different culture. He continued. I'm not racist or anything like that. I have a black friend. She confirmed. I never said you were. I just think it would be nice to see a white girl at a black party. He joked. What is there not enough black girls for you to harass? She questioned. I love women. I don't date based on the color of a woman's skin but based on her values. If she values life and its delicatessens, then we would be in perfect harmony for each other. He assured her. I'm the same way. Passion is what I yearn for. Not a big dick or an expensive car that could eventually kill both you and me. She replied.

She was now first in line. She ordered a chocolate shake and a cheeseburger with extra cheese. She paid for her order, then it was Tony's turn to order. Can I have four number 4's? With two of those I would like a chocolate shake, one banana, and one strawberry please. Also can you be light on the salt on all of those. I need lots of ketchup and hot sauce as well ma'am. He said as Elizabeth stood with her shake in her hand.

Ok your total is $24.67. Cash or credit? The woman replied. Credit. He confirmed. So maybe I will see you tonight Tisha? He said as he handed the woman the card. So you are coming tonight? She questioned as she handed him the card, the receipt, and a pen? Yea, of course! I want to know who is coming out. He said as he handed her the receipt and the pen back. I know I shouldn't be telling you this, but Kim is coming out. She said as she placed the receipt in the register. What? He said. Yea she has been on line for six months now. He responded. Why didn't she tell me? He puzzled. Because she couldn't! She acknowledged. That doesn't make any since. He pled. She will explain everything to you later I'm sure. She proclaimed.

Elizabeth stood lost at the conversation. She had no clue what the two were talking about or what to say to them. So she just stood and enjoyed her shake as she patiently awaited her food. Then a man appeared to the counter with her food. She told Tony she would catch up with him later as she walked away.

Tony was now furious. He had now just discovered that his long time girlfriend was keeping a huge secret from him. He told her everything and promised to never keep a secret from her. When Tony had met Kim, he was a player. He chose to commit to Kim and give up his childish ways. He started going to church and he started praying more often. He even got a job at Fidelity Enterprises so he could buy her an engagement ring. She was not the woman she portrayed herself to be is all Tony could think in the back of his head.

Tony stormed to the table with all the food and shakes in his arms. What's wrong with you? Trenard asked as Tony shoved the food in front of them. Man, Kim is a bitch. He replied in anger. What? Why you say that? Coolie questioned as he stuffed his face. Cause she lied to me. Tony responded as he stared at Larry. No more love man. I swear these females be acting like they so perfect and be the most foul creatures ever. Tony proclaimed. Yea man! I told you, once a dog is put in the dog pound, he always finds his way back. Larry joked as he reached to shake Tony's hand. Tony grabbed it and said d4l, dogs for life baby. The guys howled like dogs.

Shake it, shake it, shake it baby, the music roared from the house as they walked to the porch. Tupac was Sherry's favorite rapper and every time they had a party, she made sure his songs were played. Hey guys I'm going catch y'all later. Trenard said as he entered the house. Larry followed behind him. That left Coolie and Tony standing there looking lost. So what's the plan for tonight? Coolie quizzed Tony. To find the tightest pussy in here. He said as he walked into the house.

There were people everywhere you turned. The house was jam packed. Everyone was here to see the new line. It was a black college student thing that only blacks understood. All the guys would join the frats to get the girls and all the girls would join the sororities to be the most popular on campus. You pledged one of the organizations you knew people wouldn't expect you too. If you did pledge what people expected you too, everyone said it was because you were a legacy or you fit in perfectly.

REFLECTIONS

And tonight was no different than any other night, except Kim was one of those girls. He knew how much Kim wanted to fit in with everyone, but he didn't know she would keep such a secret from him. Maybe that was the real reason they broke up, because she couldn't keep it from him if they were together. He felt a bit of relief come over him as his thoughts filled his head. He finally came to the conclusion that this was the only reason she would dump him.

Hey! Larry yelled as walked towards Sherry. Hi Larry! She yelled back as she reached to hug him. I am so glad you came. She said as she lay her head in his chest. I know you really wanted me to be here, so I wouldn't miss it for the world. He told her as he gazed into her eyes. So did your boys come with you? She asked as they stared into each other's eyes. Yea they're somewhere around here. He responded. Good, Gina has been dying to get her hands on him. She joked. Who? Larry puzzled. None of your business. She answered with sass. I have something I need to tell you. Larry began. I think we should go to a more private spot than here. He said as he looked up at the ceiling. Alright, after the unveiling we will talk. She replied. How long before that happens? He questioned. Five minutes. After the last song plays meet upstairs in the third room on the right side. He answered as she left him standing.

The unveiling took thirty minutes. It was twelve of them. Their line name was the Twelve Disciples. There was Ashlei, Alexis, Moniet, Tia, Threta, Ayana, Selita, Unique, and Roberta. There was also Kim, Ericka, and Brittani, the only white girls on the line. After all them were introduced, they strolled to their national anthem. When they were done, everyone surrounded them congratulating them and offering gifts.

Larry walked up the stairs. His nerves began to take over as he got closer and closer to the door.

So you mean to tell me that you are gay? Trenard yelled. Yea, I'm sorry. I always have been. I wanted you to try to make me straight, but you didn't. She explained. Selita was from Los Angeles. She was Mexican and black. Her mother was an illegal immigrant when her father met her. After three years of dating, Selita was born. Three months after she was born, her mother was deported from the country and her father gained sole custody of her. She was caramel in complexion, about 5'4, 110 lbs, with short curly hair, and grey eyes.

Trenard and she had been dating since their freshman year at SV. Trenard cheated on her the entire time they were together. She knew of his infidelity but never admitted to it because she really didn't care. He was just a front for her. Her dad didn't approve of her being a lesbian. So she needed a guy to make her look good. Trenard was the captain of the football team, a member of Sigma Alpha Psi, had a 3.7 GPA, and worked for Fidelity enterprises. He was the perfect catch. She never told Trenard that she liked girls either. She would sit and fantasize about all the women he fantasized about.

So what am I supposed to do now? He questioned as he put his head in his hands. Marry me, you asshole. She demanded. What? He questioned as he pulled his head from his hands. We can have threesomes with other women and have a family. I'm the only woman you are going to ever meet who will want such a lifestyle. She responded. He looked confused. He didn't know whether to cry or to cheer. He loved Selita but he just liked fucking other girls. So you mean to tell me you would be ok with me having sex with another woman? He questioned. Yea as long as I can be with her too. She smiled. Well, hell yea. Let's get married. He cheered as he picked her up and kissed her.

Larry knew that this was the make it or break it moment in his life. As he twisted the knob on the door, his heart beat faster and faster. When he finally opened the door, Sherry sat there awaiting him on the bed. I thought you weren't going to show she joked as she moved towards him. He smiled and eased his way to her. When he got to her, he sat on the floor so that he could stare her in her eyes as he talked.

REFLECTIONS

He was nervous again as he sat in front of the woman he loved ready to confess. There is a lot that I have to say to you before it's too late. I hope you can forgive me and understand why I did what I did. He started. You're scaring me. What did you do? She asked as he placed his hands on her thighs. I lied about who you were and what you meant to me to the fellas. He belched out. What you mean? She questioned. I mean I told them you were my freak and that you were only a freak for me. He said as he put his head down. She began to laugh. What? I thought you were about to tell me you killed somebody. She replied. There is more. He said as he lifted his head and kneeled on one knee. Sherry Marie Jackson, I love you. There is no other woman in this world I would rather be with then you. I spend all my days and nights thinking of you and how our future could be so great. I have loved you since that day in the park when you told me that your biggest fear was not being loved. I promise I will always love you and never ever let you go. He proclaimed.

She was in awe. She didn't know what to say. She just sat there staring at him as he poured out his heart for her. Sherry was the president of her sorority, the captain of the debate team, and the leading financial officer at Fidelity Enterprises. She was a virgin saving herself for marriage. She prided herself on never giver giving it up. Larry was her everything. He was always there for her and always made her feel whole. She always had the hugest crush on him but never thought that he saw her in the same way.

So she kept it to herself. Now here he was telling her he was madly in love with her. A tear suddenly rolled down her cheek. Larry wiped it with his hand as he continued talking. She placed her hand on his mouth gesture him to be quiet. I don't care what you have said about me to your friends. Long as you tell them that we are getting married. She said as she proceeded to kiss him.

Elizabeth didn't know how to find the house. So she brought along her two friends. When they arrived at the house, the noticed how the house was overcrowded. They proceeded to walk into the house. As they entered the house, the music roared from the speakers. I'm going to try to find him guys. Wish me luck. Elizabeth yelled as she moved through the crowd. Tony was nowhere to be found.

CHARLIE KAAR

Eliza? Someone yelled from behind her. She slowly turned in the crowd to see her best friend from high school Kim. Oh My Gosh! What are you doing here? Elizabeth questioned as the two embraced each other. I just pledged this organization. I love what they stand for. She responded. Cool. Elizabeth responded. So what are you doing here Eliza? Kim puzzled. I'm here for this guy. Elizabeth responded. He must be pretty awesome to have you meeting him places. The girl I once knew made the guys chase her. She joked. The two talked a few more minutes when Elizabeth spotted Tony. Well it was good seeing you. I have to go. She said as she pushed her way through the crowd.

Tony was dancing with a girl across the room. He had been drinking and was very horny. The girl rubbed her butt all up against him. How about we go upstairs and talk? The girl whispered in his ear. Yea that sounds cool. He said as she pulled him through the crowd. As Elizabeth approached where she had once saw Tony, she noticed he was gone.

The girl shoved him on the bed and jumped on top of him. I have condoms, so we can have as much fun as you want to. She said as she kissed his neck. She had a small red dress on. She slowly kissed her way to his stomach lifting his shirt over his head. I heard you have a really big one she said as she licked his stomach.

Tony hadn't had sex since him and Kim had broken up. That was over four months ago. His manhood bulged in his pants. She noticed and unzipped his pants. Tony began to moan a little as she licked the head. He was rock hard and wanted so badly to be inside a wet, tight hole. She slowly pulled his pants down to his ankles. The she came back to his dick and began to suck it. She moved it in and out of her mouth as she stroked his balls with her fingers. After ten minutes of sucking his dick, the girl stood to take off all her clothes and Tony copied.

REFLECTIONS

She had the perfect body and so did he. She had a small waist, with a huge butt, huge tits, and a flat stomach. He had chiseled abs, an outie belly button, a nice ass, and a huge dick. As he finished undressing, he grabbed her and began to suck her tits. First he nibbled on the left nipple, slowly flicking his tongue across it as she moaned. Then he sucked the right one. As he continued sucking on her nipples, he picked her up and placed her back on the bed on her back and began fingering her. With two fingers inside of her, she began to moan louder and louder. Tony had precum just oozing from his dick. He wanted to be in her so bad. Now using three fingers, he was fingering her faster and faster. Her moaning was now even louder than before.

Tony knew that if he didn't enter her soon he would be left cuming by himself. So he reached over to the dresser drawer and grabbed a condom. He quickly put in on and moved towards her opening. He slowly pushed his way inside of her. She was so tight and wet. Tony loved the feeling he was feeling. As he pushed, she moaned and moaned. Then he was finally inside her, he be began to fuck her in a slow and gentle motion as he tongue kissed her.

She was in ecstasy. Her eyes rolled to the back of her head as he thrusted into her harder and harder with each stroke. He was fucking her so hard now. She began screaming. Tony quickly flipped her to where she was on her stomach and her head was in the pillow. He, then continued fucking her. After two hours of fucking of her, Tony was ready to cum. I'm about to cum she yelled as he stared into her eyes. He said me too as he quickly pulled out of her and took the condom off. He began to stroke his penis with his hand. I want it in my mouth she insisted, so Tony rushed to her face and started face fucking her. Then all of a sudden her mouth was filled with cum. She swallowed it all as if it were a glass of milk. Tony fell over on top of her and breathed heavily. He slowly drifted off to sleep as she put on her clothes and returned to the party.

Tony slept for another thirty minutes or so. He woke up feeling like he had just lifted a weight from his shoulders. He now longer wondered why Kim had left him. Now he thought of all the pussy he was missing out on being with her. He thought back to the days when getting ass was like scoring a touchdown. It was easy breezy for him and he had let it go for Kim.

CHARLIE KAAR

Elizabeth searched all over for Tony. Did you find him? The first girl asked as the three of them met back on the porch. I let him slip away. She responded in pain. He's cute. The second girl said as she pointed at a guy who stood talking to a female across the yard. It was Tony talking to a female. Elizabeth remembered how she always found him talking to a female and began to smirk. That's him guys. Really? The first girl asked. Yea. I guess I will see you in the morning. She signaled as she walked towards him and the girl.

I never meant to hurt you Tony. I just wanted what was best for you. The girl said before rubbing his cheeks and walking away. Kim had explained to Tony she had only broke up with him to be in the sorority. They made all the girls dump their boyfriends.

Tony didn't care what Kim had to say. All he could think about was how much pussy he could get before the sun came up. Hi stranger! Elizabeth acknowledged as she walked towards him. So you came? He questioned as he reached to hug her. Tony couldn't help but notice how good she looked. So how about we get out of here and go talk. He continued. Sure she said as she followed him through the bushes.

Tony knew that he was about to score. All he wanted to do now was bang Elizabeth until the sun came up. As the two walked, he fantasized about how he would fuck her. He even contemplated what it would be like to fuck her and her friends. Elizabeth continued talking as Tony was lost in his sexscapade. Wait, I need to go back to room to check on my friend Claudia. Elizabeth said as she came to a stop. Ok, sure thing. He quickly responded.

As they approached the house, Tony noticed how quiet it was. The two entered the house. Elizabeth led him to the back of the house to a room holding his hand. As he entered the room, she quickly turned on the lights. Tony looked puzzled when he saw no one in the room. So where is she? He questioned. She is sleeping. She answered as she pointed to a fat white cat sleeping in the far corner of the room. Oh! She is a cat. He said as he began to laugh.

As he began to sit on the bed, Elizabeth came and sat next to him. The two began kissing and fondling with one another. Slowly things led to another. Tony was deep inside her with no condom and in complete ecstasy. It's so good. Don't stop. She moaned as she dug her fingers in his back. I'm about to cum. He said as pumped harder and faster inside of her. No wait. I'm cuming too. She yelled. Then he just exploded all inside of her and collapsed on top of her. The two sat breathing very heavily in the moment.

REFLECTIONS

Elizabeth's mind raced with a million thoughts. She had never been fucked the way that Tony fucked her. He made her feel like he actually cared about her while they fucked. She didn't know what to think now, but she knew that she liked having sex with him. Over the next few days, every few hours the two met somewhere on campus to fuck. The library, The Blank's after dark, the auditorium, the registrar's office, the fountain, the bush behind Merill hall, his dorm room, and even the janitor's closet were their hook up spots. They never used condoms.

Yo, so I have something to tell you. Tony blushed as he suited up for practice. I met this girl and we be freaking every other hour. He continued. Yea, what happened with Kim? Larry wondered. We are done, the dog is back. Tony howled. Larry looked at him and began to shake his head. I have something to tell you too, bruh. Larry said as he put on his cleats. I asked Sherry to marry me and she said yes. He continued.

Tony had a puzzled look on his face. Are you serious? Tony questioned. As a heart attack! Larry replied. But she a freak though. Tony reaffirmed. She my freak and I'm going make sure it stays that way. He responded. But marriage? Don't you think you want to wait? Tony questioned. No. You wait for love and when you find it, you make it yours forever and ever. Larry said as he pulled the ring from his pocket.

Today was finally the day of the big game. Tony had spent the night with Elizabeth. They played Mango Crash until they started fucking. He woke up early that morning and ran a few laps to prep for the game. He knew that sex on game day come ruin his performance. So he tried to stay clear of Elizabeth on this day.

So guys I have someone I want you guys to meet. Larry announced as they walked to the field. Yea, If it ain't it Mariah, save her for one of your honky friends! Trenard joked as he carried the bag of balls. Shut up fag! Larry quickly yelled. It's my sister. She said I didn't have any time for her all week so she said she would meet us on the field. He continued. You have a sister? Coolie questioned. Alright, cool. Tony replied.

This is Elizabeth, Brandy, and Tiffani. Larry said as the guys approached the field. Three white girls stood there staring at the guys. Tony looked as if though he had seen a ghost. Which one is your sister? Trenard puzzled. Me, I'm Elizabeth. She answered as she reached to shake his hand.

The guys threw the balls back and forth across the field as a warm up. Tony tried not to focus on the obvious. He practiced some drills with Trenard as the three girls sat and watched. Give me twenty five suicides men. Trenard demanded as the guys reached the line. They all took off except for Tony. He said he was going to save his knee for the game.

After about forty minutes of warming up, the guys decided they had done enough. They headed towards the locker room. The ladies followed behind them. Tony went straight to the shower and showered up. Then Coolie showered and after he finished Larry showered. Trenard was always the last to shower. It was tradition for the captain be the last at everything.

Tony knew he was in trouble. He knew that if Larry found out that he had been banging his sister, he would kill him. The thought haunted him as Elizabeth stared at him. So what's up? You ready to take it the house? Larry yelled to Tony as he suited up for the game. Yea, man! Tony replied reluctantly as he suited up in his home uniform.

The girls stood to the far side of the locker room near the entrance. The two girls left Elizabeth standing there. She slowly moved towards where her brother and Tony stood talking. Well I will see you after the game. I love you. Good luck! Elizabeth yelled to her brother as she stormed out of the locker room. Love you too. He yelled as the door slammed behind her.

Tony began pacing the room. He didn't know what to do. Whether to tell Larry that the freak he had been speaking about was his sister or to just commit suicide tormented him inside. He decided he had to do what was best for him. He liked having sex with her but was sex with her worth his friendship with Larry worth it he thought. He thought of a million ways to end it with her. Then he quickly ran out the locker room to catch up to Elizabeth.

REFLECTIONS

Hey wait up! He yelled. Hi, loverboy. She replied as he walked to her. This has to end. He whined. What? She questioned. We can't see each other anymore. He said as he caught his breath. Why? Is it because I'm Larry's sister? She puzzled. Yea, he is my right hand man. I can't be getting busy with his sister. And besides I care too much about you anyway. He continued.

Elizabeth's face was now red as a stop sign. She was furious. Tony kissed on her forehead and turned and began to walk away. Tony walked away slowly with his head down. Tony really liked Elizabeth. She was sweet, loving, and considerate. She always made him feel like he was important.

As he reentered the locker room, Tony noticed he was the only one left in there. This was the last time he would play on the home field with his best friends Trenard and Larry. For the first time in his life, Tony wanted to cry. He was about to lose his girl and his friends. He kneeled down and began to pray. He prayed for the strength to win the game, to play without his boys next season, and the courage to move on from his past. As he finished his prayer, Coach Lamont walked in. Boy, come on. We have a bowl to win. He said as he rushed Tony out of the locker room.

Southern Valley won their homecoming game 57-13. Tony scored three touchdowns. Larry passed 300 yards and Trenard had twenty two sacs under his belt. After the game finished, the guys waited for the field to be cleared. So now what? Tony questioned Larry. The draft is next week and I plan on marrying the week after that. He smiled. You have to be my best man. Larry continued as the guys moved towards the lights. Yea I will be. Tony confirmed as he shook Larry's hand. Then all the lights were off on the field. The guys howled and said their goodbyes to the dog pound for the last time as they exited the field.

Elizabeth got on a plane and flew back to Virginia Beach the next morning. She stayed with her father for a few days and then flew back home to New York. When she got to the city, she met up with Turk and dumped him. He told her she was stupid and that he could have any bitch he wanted.

CHARLIE KAAR

Elizabeth was three weeks pregnant and didn't know. She only knew that she wasn't feeling well. Ugh, Ugh. The vomit streamed down her shirt as she tried to race to the bathroom. Oh my God! Are you okay? Rebecca asked. I'm fine. I just had a little too much to eat today. Elizabeth replied. Rebecca stared at Elizabeth as she leaned over the toilet. Are you pregnant? She questioned. No. Well I don't know. She replied as she held her stomach.

Eight months later Zachary Jamal Glowneic was born. When Zachary was born, Elizabeth cried like a baby. She immediately knew that he was Tony's child. The baby had green eyes, caramel skin, dark, black hair, and the softest skin. She felt like he was such a gift. She couldn't have Tony, but she could have Tony's seed. Instead of telling Tony, she decided she would keep him to herself and never tell a soul that Tony was the father.

ZACHARY

How are you doing these days Eliza? Tony questioned as he shut the door behind him. I'm fine. I've just been enjoying life. She replied as she turned to face him. So what do you think of her? He puzzled as he moved across the room. She seems like a sweetheart. She replied reluctantly. So no one knows about us? He said as he turned to face her. Not a soul. She said as her eyes began to water. What's wrong? He asked as he slowly came to hold her. I wish what we had could have been more. I really feel like you never gave us a chance because you were afraid of love. She sobbed. I was young and stupid. I want to apologize for hurting you. I never meant to hurt you. You were one of my greatest joys. He spoke as she cried in his chest.

CHARLIE KAAR

So how long have you two been dating? Rebecca asked as her and Chuchie shared some pie. A little over a year now. She replied with her mouth full of pie. Cool, he is such an awesome guy. He is going to be such a great man to you I just know it. Rebecca continued. Thanks, I just want to be the best woman for him. Chuchie replied as she finished the pie. How does it feel to be a mother? Rebecca as she looked Chuchie's figure. It's a little tiring. Every day I wake up and want to eat everything I see. Whether its pickles and milk, I just eat. Then I'm always so emotional. Chuchie replied. Wow sounds just like my sister. She has son too. Rebecca started. Zackie is what I call him. He is seven years old and thinks he is thirty. He usually spends his summer with me. She continued. Eliza is really a great mother and you will be too. She finished. Thanks. Chuchie replied as she began to get up from the table.

Eliza was now in the kitchen washing dishes. Chuchie walked into the kitchen and placed her dishes on the counter. Tony stood in the door of the refrigerator looking for the pie that Chuchie had just finished. Chuchie looked into Eliza's eyes and noticed she had been crying. Why the long face? She asked her as she helped out with the dishes. Oh my allergies have been bothering me a little. I'm fine. She replied as she glared at Chuchie.

Where is all the pie? Tony yelled as he slammed the fridge door. Sorry sweetie. It was so delicious and I couldn't control myself. Chuchie acknowledged. Tony now had a dumbfounded look on his face. He loved Rebecca's pies. He would always have two or three slices and then lick the pan. He could not believe he missed out on the pie. It's ok baby. As long as you and my son eat I will be ok. He said as he kissed Chuchie's stomach and left the kitchen. Chuchie followed behind him.

A tear rolled down Eliza's left cheek. The father of her child was soon to be married and a father to another child. The thought forced more and more tears to form in her eyes. It was very painful for her to watch the man she loved with another woman.

REFLECTIONS

Where is my boy? Mr. Glowneic puzzled as he walked in the kitchen. He's in Madrid with his nanny. Eliza answered as she continued to wash dishes. Why didn't you bring him to see his grandfather girl? He puzzled. Dad, I already told you Zack only visits in the summer. She iterated as she throw the towel down. He needs a man in his life, if you want him to be a man. He continued as he picked the towel p from the floor. I know Dad. She calmed down. When am I going to see his father? He finished. Dad, can we please discuss this another time? God! She replied as she stormed out of the kitchen.

Dinner was amazing and it was a pleasure meeting you all. I hope to see you guys again very soon. Chuchie said as she held Tony's hand. Yea thanks. I love you guys. He continued. The two gave hugs and said their goodbyes to everyone but Eliza. Eliza suddenly appeared from the other room.

Good night. It was swell meeting you honey. I wish you the best with the baby. She said as she smooch Chuchie farewell. Yea and I hope your allergies get better. Chuchie responded.

Rebecca now had a confused look on her face. Larry was allergic to wasps, bees, and pollen. Rebecca was allergic to strawberries, paprika, and peanut butter. Eliza didn't have any allergies. Her mom always noted this when they were younger. Rebecca wondered why Eliza had told such a whit lie.

Your allergies? Rebecca said as she walked into the room. Eliza was now lying down. What are you talking about? She said as she turned over. You don't have any allergies Eliza. What is your problem?

Eliza put her head down in the pillow and began to sob. What's going on? Rebecca asked as she sat next to her baby sister on the bed. My life is a complete sham. He doesn't even know. I am a horrible person. She sobbed. What are you talking about? Rebecca puzzled as rubbed Eliza's back. How I have been treating Tony for all these years. She responded. What?

Rebecca was dumbfounded. Eliza what happened? She whispered. Tony is Zach's father. What? How? Oh My God, does he know? She quickly yelled. No! Eliza replied as she turned to look her sister in the eyes. Remember Larry's last college game? Eliza puzzled. Yea! Rebecca responded in disbelief. I went a week early to get used to the campus. I met Tony and we started having sex. We never used any type of protection. He dumped me right before the game and we never touched each other again. He doesn't even know I have a child. He thinks I'm still a model. She continued as tears rolled down her cheeks.

You have to tell him and give him a chance to be in his son's life Liza. Rebecca replied as she rubbed the tears from her sister's face. I know. I just don't know how I will do it. Eliza replied Just say it. I'm sure he will understand. Rebecca stated as she walked out the room door.

Hi little man! She said through the phone. Hi mommy! When are you coming home? The young voice replied. I'm not cause Mommy wants you to come to see grandpa, your aunt, and your uncle. She gleamed. Really, I get to come to Virginia? He puzzled. Yes sweetie! In the morning you and Mrs. Flores are going to fly down here to me and I will pick you guy up from the airport. She reiterated. I love you see tomorrow! Eliza continued before hanging up the phone.

So much was to be done with so little time. Eliza was prepared t introduce Zachary and Tony, but she didn't know how she would do it. She quickly began to think of ways she could do it. Maybe we can all just sit down for lunch, maybe we can all meet Kola's Jungle and the two could play together, or maybe we can meet at his house. Many thoughts swirled through her head. Then a light bulb went off in deep inside her. She grabbed a pen and piece of paper from the dresser and began to write

REFLECTIONS

My dearest and fairest friend,

I am so proud of your many accomplishments. You are a very, beautiful human being. From the way you care for my father to the way you care for your soon to be wife and child, I applaud your efforts. It is to my understanding that you love life's blessing, so I'm sure you will clear your heart and mind and join me tomorrow for a beautiful ceremony in the honor of you and your notable accomplishments. Please meet me tomorrow at 3PM at 5897 Wilson Blvd.   Come alone and wear something casual. Don't contact me or anyone else in regards to the event. Be prepared to bring the inner kid out of you. Also, wear comfortable shoes. I look forward to seeing you tomorrow!

With Love

Rebecca Glowneic

She placed the letter in an envelope and kissed the envelope. The envelope resembled a love letter. She simply thought Tony would enjoy such a gift from Rebecca. She knew how close Tony and Rebecca were. He always talked about how he would do anything for her and Rebecca saw Tony as her younger brother. So the plan was perfect. She got dressed and went to deliver the letter to Tony.

As she pulled into his driveway, she noticed only Tony's car was home. She turned the car off and sat contemplating the next few minutes of her life. She began to feel a little light headed. She knew that if she was to do anything wrong in the next 24 hours, all her hopes and dreams would be shattered. She took the key out of the ignition and slowly got out of the car.

She was wearing her favorite Levi jeans, a black Gucci shirt, and some Louboutin pumps. She had just thrown on something out her suitcase. She was always fabulous no matter where she was going or what she was doing. This was trait she had since she was younger. During her high school years, she realized she was flawless so she started modeling.

After being a model for so many years, she was one of the industry's most respected models. She was often called *The White Naomi Campbell*. She gave up modeling after Zachary was born. She knew that if she was to continue being a model, she would never have time for her son. It was a great sacrifice for her because she loved the luxury life.

CHARLIE KAAR

When Zachary was two years old, he was offered a position to become the face of Perfect Fit, the diaper company. He modeled for the company until the age of four. In the that year of working for the company, Zachary made $3,000,000. Then at the age of four, he went on to become the face of Yo Children's Life Insurance. He continued working with this company until he was six years old. Eliza thought it would be nice for him to enjoy his childhood. Through Yo, Zachary accumulated $6,000,000 in global success.

Zachary then enrolled in school in Ithaca, New York. Eliza moved here a few months after he was born. She thought it was a great place to raise him. He enjoyed attending Fall Creek Elementary School. For the first few months of school, Eliza walked Zach to school each morning. Then he told her he was a big boy and he could walk himself. He was previously home schooled due to his very busy schedule, but he preferred to be in school where he could learn with other children.

Hey Liza! Come on in. He said as he opened the door. How are you Tony? She puzzled as she walked through the door. I'm fine; I was just getting ready to go shoot some hoops. He explained as she walked into the house. She marveled at the beautiful home and wondered if he was in love with the woman or in love with her potential.

I'm just dropping this off for Becca. She asked me to give it to you since I was headed out this way. She lied. Cool, what is it? He questioned as he looked at the lipstick stain. I don't know. I was hoping you would let me read it. She lied again. Oh so you don't know what's inside? He asked as he stared in her eyes. No I don't. She spoke. If it's from her to me, I can't let you read it. It's Dr. and Patient confidentiality. He iterated. But what if it's something I need to know? She puzzled now with a stern look on her face. It's not any of my concern to get involved in any of your family matters. He professed as he placed the letter on the table. Whatever! You will very soon. She said as headed back out the front door.

As he locked the door, he wondered what was in the letter. He sat on the couch near the table where the letter sat. He scanned the room for a quick second and then grabbed the letter and opened it so he could read it. He read the letter very carefully. After he finished the letter, he went into the kitchen. He turned on the stove and sat the letter and the envelope on the eye. It quickly caught a blaze. Tony turned off the stove and walked away as the paper sat there on fire.

Tony woke up the next morning very excited. He knew that Rebecca appreciated everything he had done for her father. He thought to himself as he brushed his teeth what she would have prepared for him.

Baby! He yelled as he walked back into the bedroom. Yes, honey! Chuchie yelled from down the stairs. He quickly headed down the stairs. I'm going to be a little busy today. I have a lot to do. He explained as he reached the kitchen. Ok. She said as she sat his breakfast on the table. The two shared breakfast and then made love on the couch. Tony then headed out for the day.

Zach! She yelled as she spotted the young man. Mommy! He yelled back as he ran into her arms. I missed you so much my love. She confessed as she spent him around in her arms. He was wearing a baby blue shirt, a pair of khaki shorts, and his favorite sneakers. He looked more and more like his father each day. He was starting to grow out and his eyes changed colors as often as it rained. Eliza stared at him for a second and saw his father in him.

It had been three weeks since the two had been united. I have a big surprise you little man. She said as she placed him back on the ground. What is it? He puzzled as he kissed his mother on the cheek. You have to wait and see. Now let's go see PaPa. She said as she started walking.

The airport was very busy this morning.   How was the flight Ms. Flores? Eliza asked the woman. Excellente! She replied. Mi madre es muy bonita! Zach quickly asserted. Gracias! El español es cada vez mejor. She continued. I see you guys have been working on a little Spanish. Liza said. Yes he wants to learn. He asked me to teach him and I said si. Ms. Flores replied as they put their luggage in the trunk of the car.

Along the car ride to her father's house, Zach feel asleep. He was exhausted from such a long flight. Eliza remembered his first time flying. He cried because he didn't want to get on the plane for two hours. After he finally got on the plane, he looked around for a few minutes. Once the plane was high in the sky, he went asleep.

The car pulled into the driveway as Zachary awoke from his nap. The airport was thirty minutes away from her father's home, so the child as well rested. They got out the car and got their luggage out.

Where is PaPa? The boy puzzled as they headed to porch. He is inside. Eliza replied. Ms. Flores, I booked you a room at the Yhing Hotel. I hope that is fine with you. She explained. Of course it is Ms. Glowneic. She replied as they entered the house. Dad! Eliza yelled through the house as she walked into the kitchen. Zach followed behind her.

The old man sat eating a sandwich at the table in the dining room. As he was getting ready to say hey, Zach ran to his PaPa. Pa, I missed you. He said as he hugged his grandpa. The old man embraced the son as if he hadn't seen him in years. The old man was so excited to see his grandson. You want a piece of my sandwich son? He asked the kid who now was sitting on his lap. Yes, may I have some PaPa? He replied. The old man broke his sandwich on half and gave his grandson a piece.

Ok, Zach. You and Grandpa can play for a little while then we have to go take Ms. Flores to her hotel. She said as she kissed the two males on the cheeks. Ok Mom! The boy replied with glee.

So Today I am going to introduce them to each other. Eliza confessed to Rebecca as she shut the door behind her. Really, are you nervous? She puzzled as she stopped reading the book she was reading. A little but I'm sure they will love each other. Eliza said as she sat in the chair next to the night stand. Do you think Tony will be a little upset? Rebecca asked. No, I think he will be a man about the situation and just accept his son. Eliza replied. Cool, so how are you going to tell Larry and Dad? She puzzled. I'm not. You are. Eliza said as she stared at her sister with a puppy dog face. No way! I'm not getting into your mess. She demanded. But Becca I need your help. Eliza whined. No! Rebecca yelled. Come on. While I'm explaining it to Tony, you can be here explaining it to them. Eliza preached. Ok, I'll do it. She said. Yayy! Eliza said with glee as she hugged and kissed her sister. But I'm only doing it cause I want us to be one big happy family. Rebecca said as she pushed her sister off of her.

A few hours later Eliza realized the time. Zach come on let's go. She yelled as she walked into the front room. Ms. Flores, are you ready to go? She continued. Yes, I am ready Miss. The woman replied as she grabbed her luggage.

Eliza, Zach, and Ms. Flores headed out the door. Ms. Flores placed her luggage in the backseat, buckled down Zach, and got into the passenger side of the car. Eliza got into the car an started driving. Within minutes of driving, Zach was fast asleep in the backseat. You know Miss? Ms. Flores began. Yes? Eliza responded while getting on the expressway. I think your son needs a man in his life. Ms. Flores finished. I know. He will have his father very soon. She responded.

REFLECTIONS

After thirty minutes of driving, they reached the hotel. I want be needing anymore services from you until we return back to New York in two weeks. I want you to take this time as a vacation. Thanks for being so great. Eliza said as she helped the woman get her luggage out of the car. The room is booked under your name. Just show your ID and enjoy your vacation. Eliza finished as the woman stood in disbelief. Are you sure Miss? The woman puzzled. Yes enjoy your trip! Eliza cheered as she pushed the woman towards the entrance of the hotel. The woman said bye and went into the hotel.

Eliza returned to the car and headed to meet with Tony. Zach continued to sleep. Eliza turned on light music in the car to keep herself awake. She had been up since nine that morning. Eliza pulled up and parked. Zach, come on let's have fun. She woke Zach up. The boy opened his eyes as his mother held him in her arms. He noticed where he was and quickly jumped from his mother's arms. They entered the building and headed towards the front desk.

How many will be joining you today ma'am? A young lady said. She looked like she could be in college. Three. Eliza replied. How many children? She asked as she typed on the computer. Two adults and one child, Eliza replied. How old is the child? The girl asked. Seven, Eliza replied as she picked Zach up. The total will be $35. The girl finished. Ok, the third person will be meeting me here. Eliza replied as she handed the woman her card and put Zach down. What is your name? She puzzled as she handed Eliza her card and her receipt. Ms. Glowneic. Eliza replied. Ok, someone will bring him to you. Enjoy your day. She finished.

Tony pulled up to the address. He looked confused. The place was Shipwrecks. It was a kid's play spot. He wondered if Rebecca was cranking him. He parked his car and turned it off. He then proceeded to go inside.

Once he was inside, he quickly noticed there was at least 100 kids inside. Kids were running, jumping, and screaming all over the place. Hi Sir, welcome to Shipwrecks. Where it's our duty to help you find your booty. How many will be joining you today? A woman in a pirate suit, wearing a patch on her left eye, and a beard said to him. I'm here to meet a Rebecca Glowneic. He replied. Ok, right this way. She said as she walked to the back. She is right over there sir.

Eliza stood at the bottom of a slide looking up. Zach was at the top getting ready to slide down when suddenly Tony appeared. Eliza?

CHARLIE KAAR

Where is Rebecca? He puzzled as he stared at the child coming down the slide. Eliza stared for a second then began to speak. She isn't here. It will just be us three today. Tony stared still confused. Ok but I thought this was a celebration. He said. It is. Tony meet Zach. She said as she picked the child up.

Zach this is your father. Eliza continued. What? Tony said as he stared into the boy's eyes. He pulled her away from the boy. What the hell is going on? He puzzled. Well you remember seven years ago right? She asked as she pulled her arm away. Yea, what about it? He asked with his arms now folded. I went home pregnant. I thought he was someone else's but as he got older he began to look more and more like you. She explained. So you mean to tell me we have a child together? He asked still in a state of shock. Yes. She replied.

I don't believe this. He said as the child stood wondering what the two adults were taking about. I have never lied to you before about anything. I even told you then I had a boyfriend. Eliza iterated. Yea, but over all of these years you forgot to mention you had a son. He raged. Eliza looked at the child for a second. He is yours. We can go get a DNA test on Monday. But look at him and tell me he doesn't look you. She reiterated.

Tony stared at the child for a few seconds. He remembered his childhood. He had short curly hair, beautiful eyes, and the smoothest skin. The child looked he had spit him out himself. Tony didn't know what to do. He does look just like me. But why did you never tell me until now? Tony asked as he stared at Eliza. Because I wanted to be sure. But he needs you now more than ever. She replied.

The two walked back over to where the child stood watching. This is my Dad? The boy questioned pointing at Tony. Yes it is. She replied as she picked him up. Tony, do you want to hold him? She asked as Tony still stood in disbelief. Sure I guess. He said as he grabbed the young man. Ok, I'll leave you two to talk for a little bit. Eliza said before walking off.

What's your name? The boy asked as he rubbed Tony's cheeks. I'm Tony. Tony replied as he put the boy down and sat down. Are you my Dad? The boy asked as he sat down like his father. Yes I am. How old are you? Tony asked. I'm seven. He replied. Do you like sports? Tony puzzled. Yea I like basketball, football, soccer, and swimming. The boy replied. Yea I played football. Tony answered. Really! He cheered. Yea! Tony confirmed.

REFLECTIONS

When you go to college, you are going to play too. Tony said. What's college? The boy asked as he sat in his father's lap. It's school. Tony responded. I go to school. The boy said a little perplexed. Yea but this is school after you finish school. Tony said as he smelled the boy's hair. Huh? The child questioned. We will talk about it later. So where do you live? Tony said. In Ithaca, New York. The boy replied. Do you like it there? Tony asked. Yes, it gets really cold. The boy answered as he looked up his father's chin. Do you want to move to Virginia? Tony puzzled. Can I? The boy asked still looking up his father's chin. I'm going to talk with your mom about it. Tony said as he stood up holding his son in one arm. Dad? The boy spoke. Yes? Tony replied now staring in the eyes of the boy. Will I get to see you from now on? The boy asked with watery eyes. Of course son! I promise I will never be out of your life again. Tony preached as he hugged the boy.

THE CONFESSION

Tony, Eliza, and Zach played for a few more hours. Then they went to get some ice cream from a small ice cream parlor down the street. It was eight o' clock and Tony knew Chanel was at home waiting for him. He said good night, gave his son a kiss and hug, and asked Eliza if he she was ok with including Chanel on everything. She said it was fine and Tony went home to explain the whole ordeal.

Tony entered the house. He quickly said a prayer and headed upstairs. He knew Chuchie would be in a state of shock just as he was. He walked into the bedroom. Chanel was lying on the bed. He could tell she was tired. He knew he had to tell her now or she wouldn't forgive him. He sat on the bed and began to rub her leg.

I just found out some potentially life altering news today. I just want you to listen to me before you say anything. He said as he stared to into the eyes of his love. What is it? She puzzled as she rubbed his back. Seven years ago when I was in college, I met a girl. She was a very, beautiful young lady. When kicked it off just hanging out and then we started messing around. In my eyes, I saw her as just a fling. She was just a girl I was sleeping around with. Then I found out she was Larry's sister, so I told her I couldn't see her anymore. She was only in town to watch Larry's last college game, which we won.

She said she understood when I told her I couldn't see her anymore and that was that. Then she returned home and she found out she was pregnant. She was under the speculation that the baby was her then boyfriend's child. As the child got older and older, she realized how much he didn't look like his father. She remembered the fling we shared and she began to notice the resemblances we shared. So I have a seven year old son by Eliza.

Baby I know that there a lot of things in our past that can make us or break us. But I want you to know I am just as shocked as you are. He continued. Tony I don't know what to say. Why would she keep it from you? Chanel said in disbelief. She did it all to protect me. He explained. Protect you from what? You have missed out on a great deal of your son's life. Chanel iterated. I know but I had so much on the line and she understood that. Tony explained. A friendship was more important than your son Tony? Chanel puzzled as she moved to the other side of the bed. That's not what I'm saying baby. I was in school and she was just a fling. She had to protect herself as well. Tony continued. But at the cost of you being a father to your son Tony. All I'm saying is she could have told you. Chanel said now staring at him.

She didn't know for sure until she got older. Tony continued. How does she know for sure now? She quizzed. I see me in him. He looks just like me. He preached. Just cause he looks like you doesn't mean that he is yours. Chanel raged. I know, that's why she wants us to come with her on Monday to get a paternity test. He said s held her hand. Us? She raged as she snatched her hand away. Yes she wants to include you on everything. Tony explained.

Wow, so she really wants you to be there. She said. Of course she does. She just doesn't want to ruin her relationship with you. She admires you. She thinks you are a brave woman. He said as he moved closer to her. Wow, Tony! This is a lot for me to take in at once. What about our son? Will he still be your concern or will you forget about him because of your innocent love child? She expressed as she stood up from the bed and rubbed her stomach. You're not being fair. Tony cried as he stood. Fair! What's not fair is that you're telling you got another woman pregnant seven years ago while I'm seven months pregnant with your son and engaged to be your wife. She raged.

The conversation ended with Chanel storming out of the room. Tony wondered should her chase after her. He felt she needed some time to cool off. She was very emotional and he didn't want to upset her even more. He loved her so much and he knew she knew this. She went for a drive he thought.

Tony knew he had to tell his family. His mother always hated hearing things from someone else about her son. She found out that he lost his virginity from his father. Tony promised his mother he would tell her everything after that. His mother was his best friend. He could tell her anything, but his Dad always judged him. He hated how much his Dad judged him for choosing a career outside of the NFL. Tony was asked to play for the Pittsburgh Steelers but turned down their offer to be a psychologist.

He grabbed the phone and called his mother. He broke the news to her and explained how it happened. The two talked for hours. She wanted to know everything about Chanel and her baby and about Eliza and Zach. She was more excited to be a grandmother than anything. She promised she would be in the life of both of her grandchildren and she also promised to be a great mother in law to Chanel. She gave him a little advice on marriage and commitment and told him to call his father.

I was just thinking about you. The voice said at the other end of the phone. Yea sorry I have been a little busy with work. Tony replied. That's ok. I know you have a lady now. His father iterated. Yea I do and I love her very much Dad. He confessed. Is she half the woman your mother is? His father puzzled. Yes she is Dad. Tony confirmed. That's good. You make sure you treat her right cause she may be the one you never know. He continued. I know she is the one. Tony started.

Dad! He changed the subject. Yes son! He yelled. I have a son. Tony said in a weary voice. You have a what? His father puzzled. I have a son. He's seven years old and he looks just like me. I want you and Mom to come to Virginia to meet him and your daughter in law. Tony finished. How can this be? His father questioned in disbelief. Dad it's a very long story. Tony said. Have you told your mother? He puzzled still in disbelief. Yes. Tony confirmed. And what did she say. He quizzed. She said she will be here on Friday. Tony said.

The phone line got really quiet as the two thought of what to say to each other. I'll be there Friday Son. The man said before hanging up the phone. Tony knew his father was disappointed. He could hear it in his voice. He just wanted to do what was right and his father couldn't see that. He hated how much his father disliked him.

Monday came and Tony was ready to find out the truth. He was so excited. Something deep down in him already knew the results of the test, but he knew Chanel wanted confirmation. He invited Shaliah along as well. This would be her first time meeting his family. He felt like everything was falling in place for him.

REFLECTIONS

I'm going to introduce you to my best friend today. Tony cheered. You are going to love her. Tony continued. Ok, I can't wait. He replied as the she sat in the passenger seat. The car pulled into the hospital parking garage. Tony parked the car and proceeded to open Chanel's door. He had told Chanel to meet him at the entrance. The two walked to where the saw a woman standing. Tony ran ahead of Chuchie, hugged, and greeted the woman. As Chuchie got closer, Tony yelled come on baby. Chanel, this is Shaliah. Shaliah Chanel. Tony introduced. The two women stared at each other as if they had seen a ghost. Hi! Shaliah responded quickly. Hi! Chanel said as she remembered the woman.

The night the two of them met, she thought she had heard of her name before. Now Chuchie stood before the woman who made her wet without knowing her whole name. She remembered Tony always talking about her. He talked about her and their relationship while they were growing up. Chanel couldn't believe what was happening.

It's a pleasure to finally meet the only other woman to have my man's heart. Chanel joked as she rubbed Tony's chest. It's great to meet you as well. Shaliah responded. You are very beautiful. Tony, why didn't you tell me she was this attractive? Chanel joked. He said you were the one. Tony I like her already. Shaliah joked as she stared at the woman as if she could eat her whole.

So I really have to know the truth and need both of you here with me. I love you guys. Tony said as he pulled the women in for a group hug. As he was letting go, he spotted Eliza and Zach. They were walking towards the entrance. He quickly ran to them and left Shaliah and Chanel standing at the entrance of the parking garage.

Hi little man! Tony said as he picked up his son. Hi Dad! I missed you! The boy replied as his father held him in his arms. I missed you too Dad.

So he doesn't know about you does he? Chanel whispered as she rubbed her belly. Of course he does! We grew up together. Shaliah explained. I just want you to know that night was a mistake. I love Tony as you can see. Chanel continued as she rubbed her ring finger. If that's what you say! So does he know about you is the million dollar question? Shaliah asked as she moved closer to Chuchie. Know what? There is nothing to know. Chanel expressed. Ok, that's fine. Shaliah said as she grabbed the woman's hand. I'm here to comfort you. Let me do that please. Shaliah finished as the two walked to where Eliza, the child, and Tony stood.

The two immediately knew the child belonged to Tony. Chanel noticed the boy's beautiful, hazel eyes. When she first met him, she said he stole her heart with his eyes. Shaliah saw his curly hair. The two stared at each other for a second then looked back at the child. He stood no taller than three feet and was an exact replica of Tony if he had been mixed.

I want you to meet a few people who are very important to your father. He said as he put his son back down on the ground. This is your stepmother, Chanel. She is pregnant with your baby brother. He continued. Hi Zach! Chanel said as she hugged the young man. I'm going to have a brother? He questioned as he rubbed her stomach. Yes, you are she said as she held his hand on her stomach. This is your aunt Shaliah. Tony continued as he pulled Shaliah towards him. Hello Zachary! Shaliah said as she picked the boy up and kissed his cheeks. Hi! He replied as Shaliah held him in her arms. Any time you ever need anything, I'm only one phone call away. She confessed as they headed into the hospital.

They entered the hospital. Tony knew it would be a long wait before the results would be revealed. Chanel and Shaliah sat on the opposite side of the room together. Shaliah helped to comfort Chanel. Chanel had begun feeling nausea when they entered the hospital. The place smelled like sour milk and old people to her. The receptionist gave her a bucket to vomit in if she had to. She vomited once as Shaliah rubbed her back and once as Tony held her hand.

They swabbed a little of Zachary's saliva and took a small amount of blood from him. The doctors did the same to Tony. Zachary immediately went to sleep after the procedure was done. He fell asleep in his mother's arms. She held onto him and kissed him as he slept. The three women, the sleeping child, and Tony sat patiently in the waiting room.

I want to change his name. Tony said as he sat down in the chair next to Eliza. What? She puzzled. I want him to have my name. I deserve that much. He explained. Ok. We have to talk it over with him. Eliza said as she looked down at her sleeping son. I know that he is mine. Tony said as he stared at the sleeping child.

Eliza smiled at him for a second and then stared across the room to look at Chanel.

REFLECTIONS

Chanel glared at the woman as if she wanted to kill her. Eliza sensed the look and quickly looked away.

How are you feeling? Shaliah whispered as she rubbed Chanel's back. I'm a little exhausted. She replied. Yea. I know this may be a little hard for you. She replied as she stared at the weary woman. Do you think this will change my relationship with Tony? Chanel asked trying to hold back tears. Of course it will be little different, but he will love you the same. She answered. I love him and I don't want to lose him. Chanel explained as she stared at her engagement ring.

The doctor suddenly appeared before Eliza and Tony. We just saw a few things we wanted to be accurate on. The tests have just been submitted to be further analysed. Your results will be ready on Wednesday at noon. You can come back then and we will have them ready for you. He said as the two parents stared at him. Thanks for your time. He finished as he shook Tony's hand.

So I guess we will be back on Wednesday. Tony said as he stood from his seat. Yea, this gives you time to get all his information together so that you can change his name. Eliza responded as she moved the child's arms around her neck. Right, do you have his birth certificate and his social security with you? He puzzled as he stared across the room. Yes, they are in the car. I will give them to you. She replied as she now stood up with the child now wrapped around her.

Do you mind if I steal your finance for a few hours? Shaliah joked as Tony stood before the two women. Of course not! Get to know her. He replied. Cool, we're going to get something to eat. Shaliah said as the two watched Chanel stand up from her chair. Would you like to hang out? She puzzled as Chanel finally stood up. Sure, I don't mind. She said as she kissed Tony on the cheek. The three of them exited the hospital and walked into the parking garage. Tony walked the ladies to Shaliah's car and kissed them farewell.

So what do you like to eat? Shaliah asked as she started the car. Anything but seafood is fine. Chanel responded as she put on her seatbelt. How many months are you? Shaliah puzzled as she glanced at her belly. I'm seven months pregnant. Chanel replied. Wow! You are really small to be seven months. Shaliah spoke as she reached a red light. Yea, it's a blessing and curse. Don't have children. Chanel said as she rubbed her stomach. I want a daughter. Shaliah started. I'm waiting to find the right person. She finished. I thought you were a lesbian. Chanel said as she stared at Shaliah. I am. Shaliah said as the light turned green. Lesbians have children all the time. Shaliah said staring at the woman. How? Chanel puzzled. Through sperm donors, adoptions, and sometimes the old fashioned way with a man. Shaliah explained. Are you not afraid of going to Hell? Chanel puzzled. He'll is not for me. It's for people who do bad things. I don't think God really cares who I sleep with as long as it is consensual and safe. She replied.

Chanel was a little ill. The baby was kicking her in the ribs. Uh! She moaned in pain. Are you ok? Shaliah asked as she rubbed Chanel's belly. She pulled the car into the Troops. Troops was a small soul food restaurant .Shaliah had went there when she first got to Virginia Beach. She loved it and she figured Chanel would as well. She parked the car and proceeded to open Chanel's door.

The place was packed as they entered. Are you ladies dining in or taking your odder to go? A woman said as the two entered. We're dining in. Shaliah quickly responded. Oh my God! You are Ms. Pallavi. The woman quickly noticed. Yes I am. Shaliah responded. It is such an honor to meet you. The woman continued. It's a pleasure to meet you too. Shaliah responded as she shook the woman's hand. My mom loved you. The woman finished. What's your mom's name? Shaliah asked. Stacy Codgewell. The woman finished.

Shaliah tried to remember where she heard of the name from. Then it hit her. Stacy Codgewell was Shaliah's campaign manager until she found out she had breast cancer. She continued to support Shaliah but had to step down due to the chemotherapy she had to undergo. Shaliah would check up on her every few weeks. Then the woman asked her to stop coming to see her and focus on her career.

Oh my God! I never Ms. Codgewell had a daughter. Shaliah spoke as she hugged the woman. Yes, there are two of us. I'm the oldest. The woman responded. I was off at college. I came back home to take care of my mom and to help out around the restaurant. She finished. You tell your mom I'm coming to see her whether she likes it or not. Shaliah finished as the woman showed them to their seats. Ok, I will, I hope you ladies enjoy your meal. The woman finished before she walked off.

So what exactly do you do? Chanel puzzled as she stared at Shaliah. I'm the director of the Virginia Beach Mental Health Center. Shaliah answered. No, that can be the reason that woman just acted the way she did. Chanel said still not impressed. Well, I'm running for mayor. Shaliah responded. That's where I knew you from. Chanel said as she looked around. Yea, I guess. Shaliah said unmoved. Why are you running for mayor? Chanel asked as a server brought the ladies some drinks. I want to make a difference for my community.

These are compliments of the owner. The server said. Enjoy. He said before walking off. Chanel ha a cup of orange juice and Shaliah had a glass of red wine. Don't worry. I will only have one glass. I know I have two lives in my hands. Shaliah said as she sipped from her glass of wine. Chanel downed her orange juice in seconds. I was really thirsty. She joked as she burped.

Why become a mayor? Chuchie asked when a server finally appeared. What would you ladies like to eat? A young woman said. She looked like she belonged on a runway. She was no taller than 5'6, 125 lbs, and had one of the most beautiful smiles ever. Shaliah noticed how beautiful she was. I will have the southern special. Chanel spoke looking down at her menu. No onions please and more orange juice. She finished. I will have the Supreme. I will have an orange juice as well. Shaliah said as she watched the woman. Chanel realized how Shaliah was staring, so she began to tempt her. How old are you? Chuchie asked. I'm twenty. She responded. You are very pretty. Has anyone ever told you to be a model? Chanel asked. Yes, but they have to go through too much. The woman replied. You could make a lot of money and travel the world. Chanel said as she handed the woman her menu. How about we talk about it later? Chanel said as she went in her purse and handed the woman a card. Shaliah sat quietly. Ok, I will call you. The woman said as she took the card.

What do you do exactly? Shaliah asked Chuchie. I help girls and women find self esteem. She replied as she pulled another card from her purse and handed it to Shaliah. The card read:

Chanel Jones
Motivational Specialist
Free Your Self, With My Help.
757-954-9042
helpmehelpyou@yahoo.com

But what exactly do you do? Each month I host a class on how to love yourself. I often have guest speakers. Every year I host a conference. The conference lasts three days. The first day we all come together for relaxation. The second day we all come and learn the twelve step rules to loving yourself and on the third day we party. It's an 18+ event. Chanel explained.

So I should get you home now. Shaliah said as she paid the bill. No, I'm. Not ready to go home. Chanel confessed. What do you want to do? Shaliah asked. Take me to your house. Chanel said as they left the restaurant.

The drive from the restaurant to Shaliah's house was about thirty minutes. They entered the house. Chanel marvelled at the home. The living area was magnificent. There were beautiful leather sofas along the walls. The theme seemed to be African colors. One was red, one was black, one was green, and another was white. The ceiling had a beautiful chandelier hanging down. There was beautiful fireplace surrounded with brick and wood. The air smelled like Florida rain. There was a huge TV sitting on the wall. It had to be at least 100 inches Chanel thought. The carpet was black and covered with a huge floor rug that had a lion pack on it.

Do you want to watch a movie? Shaliah asked as Chanel sat down. Sure. Chanel said. What kind of movie would you like to watch? Shaliah puzzled as she searched through her catalogue. I don't want to cry or be afraid to go to the bathroom. Chanel confessed as she got comfortable on the black sofa. Ok. We can watch *Two Can Play That Game*. Shaliah spoke. What's that? Chanel asked. You mean to tell me you haven't seen it yet? Shaliah puzzled as she put the movie in the VCR. No, I don't know what that is. Chanel reiterated. You are going to love it. Shaliah said as she grabbed a blanket and sat on the sofa next to Chuchie.

After the movie had been playing for an hour, Chanel went to sleep. Shaliah left her to sleep there and went to call Tony. She's asleep and I don't want to wake her. Shaliah said through the phone. Ok that's fine. I will swing by and get her tomorrow. Good night. Tony said before hanging up the phone.

The next day Tony picked up Chanel and took her home. She was so exhausted that she stayed in bed an entire day. He tried to make her eat but she couldn't eat. Serenai came over to see her and help out. She still didn't budge. She has a broken heart. Serenai said as the two sat in the living room smoking. I know, but it's from my past. I can't change it. Tony spoke. She will be ok. Just don't stop loving her the same. Serenai said as Tony passed her the blunt. I will always love her. Tony said as Serenai punt the blunt out. Good luck tomorrow. Serenai said as she walked towards the front door. Yea thanks. Tony said as she left.

REFLECTIONS

Wednesday finally came. Tony would find out today if he was truly Zach's father. A feeling inside if him hoped he was the father. He knew that his soon to be wife wanted confirmation.

Good morning baby! He said as he walked into the kitchen. No matter the circumstances, Chanel always made it her duty to have breakfast and dinner ready for him each day. She made sure that he always had a home cooked meal awaiting him unless he announced he wanted it otherwise. This morning she had his favorites. She had raisin coconut bread made from scratch, eggs Benedict, and the best porridge he ever had in his life served alongside with tea.

So good to see you guys today. The doctor said as Tony, Eliza, and Zachary walked into the room. Hi. They all said in unison. So we have your results. The doctor said as he opened a folder he had in his hand. Ok, and what exactly were the results? Eliza puzzled. Well, there is 99.9% chance that you are the father Mr. Alexander. The doctor said as he handed Tony a piece of paper. As Tony read the paper, a feeling of relief came over him. Your DNA is almost identical. The doctor continued. Thanks Doc. Tony said as he shook the man's hand. Tony kissed his son and left the hospital to tell Chanel the news.

OUR LITTLE SECRET

A lady never pays unless it's in smiles. She knew that if she was to get what she wanted, Chuchie would have to be out the way. She was stunning from toes to her cold heart. He made me this way is the only thought she had in her head.

So Tony what does she think of our son? She smirked. Tony stared at the woman for a second and began to smile. Are you asking if it is ok to have a son from another relationship? He questioned as he sipped on his drink. The music roared as the dancers moved around the building to make more money. Tony wondered why Eliza wanted to meet him in a strip club. Maybe she liked women as much as he did.

He slowly moved to the music. She noticed him enjoying himself and took the opportunity to do what she wanted. She stood from her seat and moved to where she was standing before him. He looked at her as if it was his last breath. She began gyrating her ass on his lap. At first, he moved his hands to the side but then he began to touch her as she danced. She was giving him a lap dance in a strip club.

A few songs later she decided she wanted more, so she pulled him to his feet. The two began dancing. Chuchie wasn't much of a dancer, so he they rarely went out. Eliza was everything that she wasn't. She liked to party, drink, smoke, and have a good time just as he did. She was the deep dark side of Chuchie that he longed for but knew he would never get.

Are you ok? She puzzled as she pulled his pants. Yea, I'm good. You just don't break a sweat. He joked as he continued dancing. The music seemed like it was getting louder and louder with each song. The two began sweating furiously. They loved the thrill though.

REFLECTIONS

I'm going to the ladies room. She said as she began to walk away.

He watched her as she swayed out of eyesight. He sat down and began to think of what Chuchie was doing. A part of him wanted to go home and another part of him wanted to stay and see where the night landed him.

Come back to life. She joked as she sat on his lap. What are you doing? He questioned her as he pretended not to want her on his lap. Does the man downstairs still like what he feels? She whispered in his ear. Or is it because you can't get it up for anyone other than her? She continued. I can do whatever I want when I want. He explained.

Really? Come to the room and show me. She mocked as she got off of him.

She glanced at him and grabbed her keys from where she was sitting. She looked at him once more and headed for the exit. As she walked away, He finished his last cup. He then got up and followed in her pursuit. He walked out the door. He noticed her drive past him. He wondered again should I go home or should I continue this night. He rushed to his car and started it up.

He followed her to the hotel. Eliza was staying in a presidential suit. The room had two separate rooms in one. The room had a room that looked like a child's room and a master bedroom. There were two bathrooms. One had only a walk in shower, a sink, and a toilet. The other had a huge Jacuzzi tub, a walk in shower, a his and hers sink, and beautiful view of the ocean. He knew that he would be in trouble.

The two sat talking on the sofa. Are you afraid? She joked. Afraid of what? He bluffed. Me? She quizzed. Why would I be afraid of you? He asked. Because you're so far away. Come closer, I promise I won't bite. She said. What do you want from me? He asked as he stared at her. Just some of what I've been missing out on. She dared. And what is that? He questioned as she eased closer to him. You. She continued. Wait, what are you saying to me? He puzzled. I want you. She said as she put her hand on his leg. Oh my god! Are you serious? He continued. The two made love that night. Tony woke up and crept home to his soon to be wife.

The next day Serenai and Chanel went out for a day in the city. They walked around downtown site seeing. This place looks like it has great food. Chanel said as she stared in the window of a restaurant. It was Planet Groove. It was a restaurant by day and a small lounge by night. Yea, it is a really nice place to eat. Would you like to try it? Serenai puzzled. No I will wait. Chanel replied as the two continued walking. Serenai, I am so glad you are here with me. Chanel said as she held the woman's hand. It's my pleasure. She replied as she kissed Chanel's hand.

So are you really ready to be a mother? Serenai asked as Chanel tried on a dress. Yes, it's like a dream come true. You know always wanted to be a mother. Chanel spoke as she stared at herself in the mirror. What will happen between us? Serenai asked as she stood from the chair she was sitting as she watched Chanel. Chanel stopped and stared at Serenai for a second.

I don't know. I will always love you Serenai. Chanel said as she held Serenai's hand. But you will be married to another. How can you love me the same? Serenai asked as she pulled her hand away.

I'm going to get this two sizes bigger because I plan on growing. Chanel said to the associate. That's fine. The woman responded to Chanel. I love this dress Serenai and I love the thought of getting married. It's just a sacrifice I have to make. Chanel said as the associate walked away.

Ok. Serenai said in disappointment. Chanel took the dress off. She paid for it with Tony's credit card. He always gave her the card to use but she had never used it until now. She wanted him to pay only for things that mattered most to her. That was the child that would bring into the world together and her dream wedding.

The two left the business. Chanel felt like a princess. She had ordered her wedding dress and now it was time to pick her wedding party and location. She was so excited.

Later that evening Tony and Larry went out for some drinks. Will you be my best man? Tony questioned Larry as he took a sip of his drink. Of course, it would be an honored! Larry cheered. The two sat at the bar on a Friday night. Tony said he just wanted to hang out with his friend like back in the old days. Do you forgive me for getting your sister pregnant? Tony asked as he stared at Larry. I know that you are a good man. I would have been upset if it were anybody else. I always felt like you were a brother and now you are. Larry explained. Tony felt relieved. The two had a few more drinks, said their goodbyes, and went home to their women.

Chanel didn't know what to do. She loved Serenai but she also loved Tony. Serenai was her best friend and lover. She decided she would express herself through a letter. She remembered how Serenai always loved it when she wrote to her. She got up out of bed and went downstairs. She went in the kitchen and went into the drawer where she kept paper and pen. She then began to write;

Sunflower Serenai,

I should quit you, but you always ease the pain. You make me feel like there are no worries. I know that I love you but I live him more. There are always ways to quit a bad habit, but you I seem to not be able to shake. You're trust and guidance I yearn for. After all these years, I can't believe I still love you. You are like vanilla to my tea to soothe my throbbing throat. You are like the sweet melon dew on my skin, always radiant. That's why I'm so torn between what I need to do. I hope you will understand the words that I am writing to you are out of love and admiration. I also believe that you came back in my life to open a door that I never thought I could open. I must let you know I am going to marry him. I hope that you will still love me the same. I just have to have security for my family. I know you may hate my decision but I will still love you the same. I just hope you are ready and willing to accept me and my husband as yours.

Your heart and soul will keep a fire a blaze in my heart forever.
Love Chanel

Shaliah and Chanel were hanging out. Chanel wanted Shaliah to help plan her wedding. The two walked into the lobby of a magnificent hotel. The ceilings had chandeliers throughout the entire hotel. The marble floors were decadent. The conference rooms were large enough to seat 500 people. The restrooms were laced with refreshments to help you use the bathroom. They had twenty stalls and each had a changing room for mothers to change their children. The fitness room sat right next to an indoor pool. The outdoor pool had a Caribbean theme. There were rocks and cliffs to jump off into the pool. There were two Jacuzzis. One sat near the shallow end and had an USB hook-up for guest to play their music on sound system. The second was near the deep end. It had a spot for guest to sit their drinks as they enjoyed the warming sensation of the Jacuzzi.

This place is perfect. We have been to a few different places all day but I think this one has my heart. Chanel cheered as a receptionist showed them around. It is pretty awesome. Shaliah reiterated as she glared at the ceilings.

Chanel was so excited. She knew Tony would love the place. She had to pee so bad. It was crazy. I think I should let you know the truth. Shaliah said as she stared at the woman. What's the truth? Chanel puzzled as she eased her way closer to her. I think I love you. Shaliah confessed. What? Are you sure? Chanel said in disbelief. You're the most wonderful person I ever met in my life. I trust you with everything including my heart and soul. Shaliah continued. I love you. She finished.

Chanel sat in a daze for a second. She didn't know what to say. A feeling within her felt like she should tell Shaliah how she felt as well. She loved her too but she didn't want to make Shaliah feel like she would love her more than Tony.

Serenai and Ce Ce are going to meet us for lunch in thirty minutes at Chato. We should get going. Chanel said as she snapped out of the daze. The two sat in silence as Chanel drove to Chato. Chanel hoped Shaliah wouldn't mention anything else about her love. Shaliah wondered if Chanel just didn't want her the way she thought she did.

The two finally reached the restaurant. Reservations please! The hostess spoke to the two lovely women as they entered the restaurant. We are here for Serenai. Chanel replied. Right this way. The hostess said as she took the two to where Ce Ce and Serenai were already seated.

Oh my God! Ce Ce said as she stood from the table to greet Chanel. You are so precious she said as the two shared smooches on the cheeks. Serenai followed behind smooching both Shaliah and Chanel. This is Shaliah. Chanel expressed as Shaliah and Ce Ce smooched each other. And you already know Serenai. Chanel finished as they all sat down.

So is the baby kicking you in the ribs yet? Ce Ce joked. Not yet, he's being good today. Chanel replied. I ordered you some orange juice and you a martini. Serenai said as the waiter brought their drinks. Thanks. The two said in unison. So I am the maid of honour is what I was just telling Serenai. Ce Ce said as she sipped from her glass. Of course you are. Chanel reiterated as she stared at Serenai. Oh, I have something for you Serenai. Chanel said. Let me give it to you before I forget. Chuchie finished as she handed her an envelope from her purse. Serenai stared at the envelope and looked back over at Chanel. What is it? She puzzled. Open it later. Chanel said as she stared at Serenai.

Are you sure you are ready to get married? Shaliah asked. Yes I am sure. Chanel answered. Ok so what colors are you seeing? Ce Ce asked. Blue and white. Chanel spoke as she nibbled on a piece of chicken. Of course! Ce Ce said as she remembered Chanel's favourite color. So we are going to take you to Vegas for the weekend if that is ok with you. Serenai said staring at Chanel. For what? Chuchie puzzled. They have this really awesome spa there that we want to treat you to and when we get back we are going to have a rehearsal. Serenai finished. Oh that sounds nice. Chanel said. Your mom, B, Kim, Stacy, Shaliah, and, Serenai, and I will all be coming with you. Ce Ce said as she held onto Chanel's hand.

So when are we going? Shaliah asked. Tomorrow? Wait, we are leaving tomorrow? Chanel asked. Yes we are sissy. B said as she walked to the table with her mother. Oh my God! Chanel said as she jumped up and hugged her sister and her mother. Ce Ce did this didn't she? Chanel asked as they all sat down. I was thinking this is too many chairs when we sat down. Shaliah said. They all began to laugh. Momma I miss you so much and you too B. Chanel said. We just want you to know how proud we are of you. Her mother said.

The ladies finished their meal and headed to Chanel's house to meet with Tony. So we are going to Vegas. Chanel said to Tony as he sat down. Yea I know. He said as she sat next to him. So Tony knew too. She asked. Yea we had to include him on the plans. B said as she ate from a bowl of chips. Yea, he is technically your husband. Ce Ce spoke. I didn't know about any of this. Shaliah said as she drink a glass of wine. And he is the one paying for everything. Serenai said as she looked at Tony. Are you really baby? Chanel asked as she leaned on him. Yea, anything for you. You don't even have to ask. I know you needed some pampering. It's been very stressful for you so go and enjoy yourself. He said before kissing her on the cheek. Awe! All the other ladies in the room said in unison.

The next morning all the ladies met with Tony and Chanel at the airport. So are you guys prepared for one of the best trips of your lives? Ce Ce asked as the ladies were still half asleep. Have a great trip! Tony said as he kissed Chanel, her family, and friends goodbye.

On the flight, all the ladies slept except Shaliah and Chanel. Why are you not asleep? Shaliah questioned. I'm so anxious. Chanel spoke as she stared out the window. Shaliah and Chanel were seated next to each other. Ce Ce and Serenai sat three rows behind Chanel and Shaliah. B and her mother were seated directly behind Ce Ce and Serenai.

Yea, marriage. Shaliah said dreadfully. It can't be that bad. Chanel said as she grabbed Shaliah's hand. I just feel like I will never be married. No one wants to marry someone like me. She said with tears in her eyes. That's not true. You just haven't met the person yet. Chanel said as she wiped a tear from Shaliah's eye. The two talked about everything from politics, religion, sexualities, and their favourite celebrities the entire flight.

Guys time to have fun! Ce Ce yelled in excitement as the ladies walked through the Vegas airport. We should take a nap first. Chanel said as she came to a stop. All the ladies stopped and stood for a second. We will not be able to sleep this trip. Serenai said as she walked next to Chanel. Chuchie, are you ok? B asked as she rubbed her sister's stomach. I'm fine. I just need a nap. Chanel answered. Ok, well let's go take a nap. Shaliah said as she grabbed Chanel's luggage and guided her towards the exit. She only can sleep for a few hours and then she has to be up Sha Sha. Ce Ce said as the ladies followed behind Shaliah and Chanel.

The ladies grabbed a cab and headed to the Yoto Resort. They all checked in. B and her mother were staying in the same room. Ce Ce and Serenai were staying in a room together. Shaliah and Chanel had a penthouse suite. There was a bedroom and a front room. The bathroom had a toilet, a vanity tub, and marble floor pattern. It also had a view the city lights. I guess I'll take the front room. Shaliah said as she placed their luggage in a closet.

After a few hours of relaxing, the ladies hit the strips. They shopped and ate in many different places. Shaliah and Chanel were getting closer and closer. They walked around holding hands and whispering secrets in each other's ears. Serenai noticed and began to feel a little jealous.

So guys I have an announcement. Chanel said as she stood from her seat. I have decided Sha Sha is going to be Jamal's Godmother. Chanel finished. When did you make this decision? Ce Ce asked angrily. I didn't do it alone. Chanel replied as she sat back down. I bet you didn't. Serenai mumbled under her breath. As you all know

REFLECTIONS

Tony loves her like a sister and she has been nothing short of a blessing since she has come into my life. She was there for me when I got the terrible news. I can't think of anyone else to be there. Chanel stated. So Tony wants this? Ce Ce asked. We both want her to be the Godmother. Will you be the Godmother of Jamal? Chanel puzzled as she stared at Shaliah. Of course! Shaliah said.

I need a drink. Serenai said as her and Ce Ce sat angrily. Yea, this really sucks. She doesn't even know her. Ce Ce said as she sipped from her glass. Serenai? Ce Ce whispered. Yes Ce Ce. Serenai replied. I think Chanel has a little crush on Shaliah. Ce Ce joked as the two stared at Chanel and Shaliah staring into each other's eyes. The ladies finished their meals and drinks and headed back to their hotel rooms.

I'm really exhausted. Chanel said as Shaliah opened the door. Me too! Shaliah replied as she flopped on the sofa. I'm going to take a bubble bath. Chanel said as she walked into the bedroom. Ok, goodnight. Shaliah yelled. Shaliah fell asleep on the sofa as Chanel took a bath. She woke up in the middle of the night and went and got in the bed with Chanel.

What are you doing? Chanel asked. I'm trying to get some sleep. Shaliah said as she got under the cover. This isn't right. Chanel said as she sat up. I'm not here for you. I'm here for the bed. Don't flatter yourself. Shaliah said as she turned to face the opposite way of where Chanel sat.

The next day ladies enjoyed brunch at the spa. They were served a full course meal with margaritas and tequilas on the side. Chanel had her usual orange juice. Then the ladies were taking to a sauna room. They all sat in the sauna making jokes an reminiscing about their past lives. Then they were given massages by heft men and towels.

So this our last night here and I just want to thank you guys for giving me the best bachelorette party ever. Chanel said as al the ladies sat around in the penthouse suite. You are the best friend a person could ever have and I love you so much. Ce Ce sid with a glass in her hand and a tear in her eye. To show you our gratitude and appreciation, we have a surprise for you. B said. Then suddenly the lights in the room were turned off and music beamed around them. Then the lights flickered on and off. Then a man stood in front of Chanel.

Woah! Where did you come from? Chanel puzzled. I hear that you are getting married. The man began as he held Chanel's hand. Yea

I am. She replied. The others sat in awe as if they knew what would take place next. He immediately began taking off his clothes. I hope this will change your mind. The man said as he began dancing to the music. Chanel cheered as the man waved his manhood in her face. Then more men appeared and they all began stripping. The ladies got a striptease from a total of five different men.

Whose idea was this? Chanel said as she shut the room door behind the last dancer. Ce Ce! Everyone in the room yelled as they pointed at her. All of y'all are sell outs! She yelled. Oh my God, we can't ever tell Tony about this. Chanel said as she hugged her best friend. He would have a fit. Shaliah said a little tipsy. I know. Chanel said as she sat next to the slurring woman. But did you enjoy yourself? Serenai puzzled with a bottle of champagne in her lap. Yes! Chanel screamed in joy. Alright time for bed! We have a plane to catch in the morning. Her mother began. They all left Shaliah and Chanel to sleep.

You will soon be Mrs. Tony Alexander. Shaliah spoke as she laid down. I know and I can't wait. Chanel said as she closed her eyes.

THE BIG DAY

This is the list for the groomsmen. Tony said as he handed the wedding planner the paper. I want everyone to be seated in alphabetical order after the direct family has been seated. Chanel said as she looked over Tony's shoulder.

We can practice it one more time and then we can leave guys. Chanel said as everyone groaned. We have already practice it a billion times Chanel. Ce Ce said as she stared at the clock on the wall. She is like the bride from hell. Serenai whispered to Shaliah. Shaliah began to giggle. No, no, no. You too are not supposed to be next to each other. Chanel yelled as she separated Serenai and Shaliah. Tony tell your friends to act right. Chanel yelled to Tony as he sat watching. Guys come on so we can go. He said.

This was the fifth rehearsal Chanel had. Everyone was exhausted. She yelled and screamed most of the time. She rearranged the seating chart thirty times before it was finalized and she changed the menu twelve times. Her mother said if Chanel gets divorced and gets married again, I'm not coming.

After two more hours, Chanel was finally satisfied with the way her wedding would be. Don't have too much fun at this party now boys. Chanel said as the fellas cheered. I will see you tomorrow baby. Tony said as he kissed her the cheek. Goodnight baby. Sha Sha make sure my woman is ok. Tony whispered to Shaliah before leaving. Serenai overheard the conversation and decided to take matters in her own hands. So Chanel, are you coming over tonight? Serenai whispered in Chanel's ear. Yea sure. Chanel said as Shaliah walked over to where the two stood talking.

So come on so I can get you home. Shaliah spoke. Did Tony put you up to this? Chanel asked as she licked her lips and glanced at the woman's body. No I just want to make sure my Godson is ok. Shaliah lied as she rubbed Chanel's belly. She will be fine… Serenai started. It's ok Serenai. I'm going home with Shaliah. Chanel cut her off as she held Shaliah's hand. Are you sure? Serenai puzzled in disbelief. Yes, I will be fine. Chanel spoke before Shaliah and she walked off.

Serenai was heated. She wanted Chanel to come back over her place so they could make love. She remembered how Ce Ce said Chanel had a crush on Shaliah. She thought of how Shaliah would be making love to her that nigh instead of her. She immediately began to plan her revenge.

She was finally ready to fit into the dress. She was getting married to the man of her dreams just weeks shy of the birth of their son. This was the day she had dreamed of for a very long time. All of her family was there to see her off and Tony's mom and dad were both there to support their son.

How are you feeling? Her mother asked as she walked into the room. I'm feeling like I finally am at peace. She said as she stared at her belly in the mirror. Baby you are so beautiful. I just want you to know how proud I am of you. Her mother started as she stood next to her daughter. I love you so much Mom! Chuchie confessed as she kissed her mother on the cheek. I love you to baby.

Now you listen to me. She continued. Yes ma'am. Chuchie replied. You better love and cherish this man forever. This what you are about to embark on is not a game. This is the work of God and no one can take this asunder. Her mother finished.

Thanks Mom. I am so glad you are here. Chanel replied as she gave her mother a hug. Chanel's mother left her in the room to herself. She now stood alone with her thoughts. She quickly kneeled down and began to pray:

REFLECTIONS

Father if this is not what you want for me, send me a sign. I only want to serve and honor you. I never want to get lost in this ever changing world. I love this man with all my heart and I know he loves me. If it is meant to be, I couldn't have asked for anything different. I want you to bless this child inside of me, the people who will be gathered today to witness such a miracle, and the man who you have sent to me. I pray that I continue to have the courage to be the perfect mother to my son and the perfect wife to my husband. I pray that no matter what he may do, I may have a heart filled with unconditional love and acceptance. I pray that he will continue to be patient with me and my brokenness. I pray that you will give this matrimony your blessing. I pray all these things in your son Jesus Christ name.

Amen

As she was getting up from her knees, someone knocked on the door. Who is it? She yelled as she caught her breath. Tiffany! The voice yelled back through the door. It was her stylist. Chanel immediately went and opened the door and let the woman in. The woman immediately came and began to prepare Chanel for the aisle.

First, the two squeezed Chanel into her dress. The dress was a maternity size so she could fit into it. Then, the woman put shoes on Chanel. Chanel just laid back on the bed as she put the shoes on her. They were a perfect fit. Chanel ordered the shoes two sizes larger six months ago. She knew her feet would get bigger. Then she did her hair. Chanel was told to wash her hair the night before and to let it air dry. The woman quickly began styling Chanel's dreads in a bun. She was slowly come to form.

It was now ten thirty. Chanel was due to walk down the aisle at ten forty five and she still wasn't ready. Her make-up was the last step. The woman quickly applied make-up on her. Chanel felt like a queen that day and she loved it.

Someone began knocking at the door. Chanel it's time for you to start walking down the aisle. Her mother yelled as she walked through the door. Yes ma'am. I'm coming. She responded.

The hotel was the perfect place for a wedding. Chanel picked the place because of the beautiful deck that led straight down to the beach. The wedding was being held on the beach. All who were in attendance were seated in beautiful chairs near the water. Chanel, the bridal party, and the groomsmen were all to stand within inches from the shoreline. Chanel had dreamed of a wedding like this one and Tony was about to fulfill her dreams.

Chanel began walking down the aisle. Her dress was very beautiful. She walked with so much grace down the aisle as Shamar and Lannie walked ahead her. Lannie was such an elegant flower girl and Shamar was the perfect ring bearer.

Tony stood before her with tears in his eyes as she walked down the aisle. The day that he never thought would happen to him was now happening. His beautiful woman was about to be his wife and the mother of his son. She was perfect and the wedding was perfect.

The bridesmaids all wore beautiful blue dresses. The groomsmen all wore black suits, white shirts, and blue ties. Larry, Trenard, Coolie, and Trenton stood beside Tony. Sierra, Serenai, Shaliah, and Kim stood beside Chanel. The pastor began speaking.

Dearly beloved, we are gathered together here in the sign of God and in the face of this company to join together this man and this woman in holy matrimony, which is commended to be honorable among all men; and therefore is not by any to be entered into unadvisedly or lightly but reverently, discreetly, advisedly and solemnly. Into this holy estate, these two persons present now come to be joined. If any person can show just cause why they may not be joined together, let them speak now or forever hold their peace. The audience remained quiet.

Marriage is the union of husband and wife in heart, body and mind. It is intended for their mutual joy and for the help and comfort given on another in prosperity and adversity. But more importantly it is a means through which a stable and loving environment may be attained. The pastor continued.

Through marriage, Tony and Chanel make a commitment together to face their disappointments, embrace their dreams, realize their hopes, and accept each other's failures. Tony and Chanel will promise one another to aspire to these ideals throughout their lives together through mutual understanding, openness, and sensitivity to each other.

REFLECTIONS

We are here today before God because marriage is one of His most sacred wishes. We are here to witness the joining in marriage of Tony and Chanel. This occasion marks the celebration of love and commitment with which this man and this woman begin their life together. And now through me He joins you together in one of the holiest bonds.

Who gives this woman in marriage to this man? He asked.

I Do, her brother spoke.

The ceremony of marriage in which you come to be united is one of the first and oldest ceremonies in the entire world, celebrated in the beginning in the presence of God himself. Marriage is a gift in that we give ourselves totally to one another. I believe that marriage is a gift given to comfort the sorrows of life and to magnify life's joys. Marriage is the clasping of hands, the blending of two hearts, the union of two lives into one, and your marriage must stand, not by the authority of the State, nor by the seal on your wedding certificate, but by the strength and power of the faith and love you have in one another. The pastor preached.

Now, will you please pass your flowers, turn and face one another and join hands to express your vows of love and devotion each to the other.

Tony turned and faced his love. He began to speak.

I'll love you until the sun falls out the sky. I'll hold your hand even if God tells us our love will not survive. I will cherish every second and every day I spend with you. I will build a monument to show how much I love you. I will write a book and the pages will be filled with the gazillion ways that I love you. I will kill the president, the pope, and even Jesus if they ever tried to come in between us. I would drink poison just so that I could hold you every day. I'll walk across the Sahara. I'll write you a love letter every day. I'll erase my heart and let you draw a new one. I'll join the military, shave my head bald, and get poked in

the butt just to take care of you. I'll create a cure for cancer, AIDS, the common cold, and anything else just to keep you in my life.

Chanel teary eyed spoke:

I will be your all. I will catch you if you should fall. I will answer every time you call. I will cook, clean, and cherish you. I will do whatever you need me to. I will always have time. I will always make sure for you and only you I will be fine. I will be wrong just so you will feel right. I will be the best mother to your kids. I will make sure that for you and our family we forever live. I will be your everything. I will be and am the woman of your dreams.

The pastor continued:

Will you please repeat this vow to Chanel saying after me: I Tony take you Chanel, to be my wife, to have and to hold from this day forward, for better or for worse, for richer or for poorer, in sickness and in health, I promise to love and cherish you.

Will you please repeat this vow to Tony saying after me: I Chanel, take you Tony, to be my husband, to have and to hold from this day forward, for better or for worse, for richer or for poorer, in sickness and in health, I promise to love and cherish you.

The word of God tells us what love is like and what love does: Love is patient; love is kind, love is not jealous. Love does not brag and is not arrogant. It does not act unbecomingly. It does not seek its own, it is not provoked, and it does not take into account a wrong suffered. It does not rejoice in unrighteousness, but rejoices with the truth, for love bears all things, believes all things, hopes all things, and endures all things, but above all, love never fails. He carried on.

Having this kind of love in your hearts for one another, you have chosen to exchange rings as the sign and seal of the promises you are making to one another today.

Do you have a ring for Chanel? He asked Tony. May I have the ring? Tony handed him the ring.
Do you have a ring for Tony? He asked Chanel. May I have the ring? Chanel handed him the ring.

REFLECTIONS

Rings are very large in their significance. They are made of a precious metal and precious stone, and that reminds us that love is not cheap or common; but indeed love is very costly and dear to us. These rings are also made in a circle and their design tells us that we must keep love continuous throughout our whole lives even as the circle of the ring is continuous. As you wear these rings, whether you are together or apart for even just a moment, may these rings be a constant reminder of the promises you are making to one another this day. He preached.

Tony, will you please take this ring and place it upon the third finger of Chanel's left hand, and holding her hand in yours, please repeat this promise to her saying after me: With this ring, I seal my promise, to be your faithful and loving husband, as God is my witness. Tony followed.

Chanel, will you please take this ring and place it upon the third finger of Tony's left hand, and holding his hand in yours please repeat this promise to him saying after me: With this ring, I seal my promise, to be your faithful and loving wife, as God is my witness. Chanel followed.

Chanel and Tony, you have come here today before us and before God and have expressed your desire to become husband and wife. You have shown your love and affection by joining hands, and have made promises of faith and devotion, each to the other, and have sealed these promises by the giving and the receiving of the rings. Therefore, it is my privilege as a minister and by the authority given to me by the State of Virginia; I now pronounce that you are husband and wife. Tony, you may kiss your wife.

Ladies and gentlemen, please welcome Mr. and Mrs. Tony Alexander. The pastor finished as the two finally stopped kissing.

The wedding was over. Chanel had her dream wedding her dream. The ceremony after was just as amazing as the wedding. Music played and both her family and Tony's family enjoyed themselves.

CHARLIE KAAR

I am so tired baby. Chanel said as she sat into her husband's lap. The music roared. I love you Mrs. Alexander. He said as he smooched her on the cheek. I love you too. She said as Serenai and Shaliah walked towards them. So guys, what's next for the newlyweds? Serenai quizzed as she sat across from where they sat. Sleep! Chanel yelled. We won't be able to sleep in the Bahamas baby. Tony said as Shaliah sat down behind the two newlyweds. Bahamas? Chuchie asked. We're going to the Bahamas if that's ok with you. Tony said as he stared into Chanel's eyes. What about the baby? Jamal doesn't need to be traveling right now. Chanel said as she held Tony's head. Oh my God! You guys are going to the Bahamas? Shaliah cheered. Yea. Tony said as he turned to face her. My baby always wanted to go, so why not? He spoke as Chanel kissed his neck.

I haven't even packed yet. Chanel realized as she stood from Tony's lap. It's ok Serenai packed for you. He said as he looked over at Serenai. Yea, surprise Chuchie. The woman said as she stood to hug her. Wait, you packed my stuff? Chuchie puzzled as she denied Serenai's hug. Yea. What's wrong? Serenai puzzled. So you knew and you didn't tell me? Chuchie spoke as she eyed Serenai. Yea. Tony said he wanted you to go to the Bahamas and he asked if I would pack your stuff. Serenai explained. Ugh, I hate you guys! Chanel raged as she stormed off.

She will be ok. Shaliah spoke before she followed behind Chanel. Chanel went into the bathroom. She felt light headed. She was very angry but happy at the same time. She rushed into a stall. As she was shutting the door, Shaliah appeared. Are you ok? Shaliah asked. I'm fine. Chanel said as she eyed her. Ugh Ugh Ugh. Throw up streamed down Shaliah's dress. Chanel turned and kneeled down over the toilet. This is really gross! Shaliah yelled as she looked down at her dress. The dress was covered in red, green, and pink vomit. What did you eat? Shaliah puzzled as she rubbed Chanel's back. I don't know. Chanel said as a tear fell from her eye. I'm ok. It's just a little morning sickness. She continued.

Why are you so upset about the trip to the Bahamas? Shaliah asked as she kneeled down next to the vomiting woman. Chanel sat down on the floor and stared at Shaliah for a second. I'm not mad about the trip. I'm mad cause Serenai knew before me. She said. But she's your best friend. Of course she is going to know. Shaliah said as she pushed Chanel's hair behind her ears. You don't understand. Chanel said as she began to pull herself up.

REFLECTIONS

I just want to be happy. Is that too much to ask for? Chanel said as Shaliah stood beside her in the small stall. No. You will be even happier in a few months. Shaliah spoke as she rubbed Chanel's belly.

Let's get back out there. Shaliah said. But what about your dress? Chanel puzzled as she eyed the streams of vomit on the dress. I'll go change. Shaliah spoke as she stepped out of the stall. Now come on Mrs. Alexander. Shaliah said with her hand stretched out for Chanel to grab. The two walked out of the bathroom.

Shaliah snuck out of the room and headed to her car. She had brought an extra pair of clothes just in case something went wrong. Her car was parked at the back of the hotel. She stuck her key in the driver side. The back door lock popped open. She bent over to get her bag of clothes. You are quite a lady. A voice from behind her said. She turned around. Oh my God! You scared me Serenai. Shaliah said as she grabbed the bag from the backseat and shut the door. Do you smoke? Serenai asked as she lit the blunt she had in her hand. No not really. Shaliah responded. What does that mean? Yes or no. Serenai asked as she moved closer to Shaliah. I haven't smoked since college. Shaliah responded as she leaned on the car. Yea. That's good. You want to hit it? Serenai asked as she held the blunt out. Shaliah stared for a second. Why not? She said as she took the blunt. She began coughing after three pulls. Take it slow. This right here is stronger the salt at the beach. Serenai said as she took the blunt back.

The two sat in Shaliah's car for another thirty minutes. They got high and talked about life. So you running for mayor I hear. Serenai said as Shaliah passed her the blunt. Yea, I am. Shaliah coughed. Why are you running? Serenai asked as she passed the blunt back. I feel like it's time for a change. You know. Shaliah responded in between puffs. I guess you are right. Serenai said as she got the blunt. They had smoked three blunts.

What the hell are you two out here doing? Tony scared the women. Why are you sneaking up on us like that? Serenai asked as she opened the back door for him. He got into the car. Let me hit the blunt. He said as he shut the door. Serenai passed him the blunt. Tony, you smoke? Shaliah asked as she turned to face him in the backseat. Only when necessary. He said as he puffed the blunt. Yes he smokes. We smoke all the time. Serenai said as Tony passed the blunt to Shaliah. Does Chanel know? Shaliah asked. Yes, she says it's ok as long it doesn't have an effect on our relationship. He said as got comfortable. Wow! I never knew. Shaliah said as she puffed on the blunt.

The three sat in the car. It was now filled with smoke. So Tony would you eat a cat's ass for a million dollars? Serenai puzzled as she passed the blunt to him. Hell yea. I have two kids and a wife to take care of. He said. The three all began laughing. We been out here a long time. You think somebody noticed we gone? Shaliah puzzled as she finally began to take the dress off. I don't know. Serenai said. I think it's only been fifteen minutes since I got out her. Tony said. Ok finish it so we can go back in. Shaliah said as she pulled her shirt over head.

Tony puffed on the blunt one time and threw it out the window. Alright. Let's go. He said as he opened his door. The three walked back into the hotel high. The music was still blasting. It was now twelve in the morning. Where have you guys been? Chanel asked as they walked to the bar. We were just chilling. Serenai lied. You look like you are high. Chanel said as she walked closer to Serenai. Tony, are you high? Chuchie puzzled as she moved away from Serenai. No just a light buzz baby. He said as he kissed her on the cheek. I want to get high too. Chanel said as she pushed him away from her. You can't. It will hurt the baby. Shaliah declared. So you're high too I bet. Chanel said as she looked at Shaliah. No, I'm just trying to help you. Shaliah lied. You're not smoking with my child in you. Tony said as he bent over kissed Chanel's belly.

I'm going to the room. Chanel said as she stared at Serenai. I will walk you up. Serenai said as she grabbed Chanel's hand. Tony, enjoy yourself! Cause tomorrow you aren't smoking anymore. Chanel said before kissing Shaliah on the cheek goodnight. Her and Serenai headed towards the elevator. Are you tired? Serenai asked as the women entered the elevator. I want to take a bubble bath. Chanel replied as she pressed the twelfth floor button. Ok. Serenai said. The elevator reached Chanel's floor after two minutes.

REFLECTIONS

The two women walked down the hall. Then they reached Chanel's room. Will you stay with me for a while? I don't want to be alone. Chanel confessed as she opened the door. Are you sure that's what you want? Serenai asked as Chanel walked through the door and turned to face her still standing on the outside. You know what I want Serenai. Chanel said staring at Serenai as she was going to eat her alive. Ok. Serenai said as she walked into the door. Go get our bath ready. Serenai said as she slapped Chanel's butt. Ok. Chanel said as she kissed Serenai. Chanel went to the bathroom. She turned on the bath water and began to undress. When the tub was half way filled, she slowly got into the water.

Serenai popped open a bottle of champagne and began to drink from it. She then proceeded to the bathroom with the bottle in her hand. As she entered the bathroom, she noticed Chanel's dress on the floor. She looked over at the tub and her hormones began to race. She shut the door and locked it. She began to take her dress off. No no. Chanel said as the woman was taking off her dress. Tease me. Make me beg for it. Chanel said seductively.

Do you want it? Serenai started as Chanel touched herself. Yes. She replied. Serenai eased her clothes off and slipped into the tub with Chanel. How long can you hold your breath for? Chanel asked as she pulled Serenai closer to her. As long as you want me to! Serenai said as she went under water. She began licking and fingering the woman. Chanel moaned as she experienced ecstasy.

After three minutes under water, Serenai came back up. The two began kissing. Serenai kissed and sucked on Chanel's ears. Chanel caressed Serenai's body. Chanel began to finger Serenai as she sucked and licked her breasts. Serenai laid her head back and moaned. Do you want to feel my tongue? Chanel whispered in Serenai's ear. Yes, please. She replied. Chanel went under water. She fingered and licked Serenai's clit.

The two decided to take it to the bed. Are you ready for this? Chanel asked as she pulled a dildo from the drawer. Serenai spread her legs open as Chanel licked up her thighs. Chanel began slowly easing the dildo inside of Serenai. You're so wet and so tight. Chanel spoke. Serenai moaned more and more. Then after a few minutes, Serenai began licking and sucking on Chanel. She wrapped her leg around her body to keep Chanel from squirming. She then inserted the dildo in her. She pushed it in deeper and deeper as Chanel moaned. Then the two did a sixty nine. Serenai lied on top of Chanel. The two licked and fingered one another. I'm about to cum! Chanel yelled. Serenai quickly got off of Chanel. Then they held each other for a few minutes as they came. The two took a shower and made love again. Then they got dressed and laid down.

As Tony entered the room, he turned on the lights. He noticed Serenai and Chanel were in the bed fast asleep. They were snuggled up with each other. He turned off the lights. He got undressed and got in the bed with them. Chanel was on the outside, Serenai was in the middle, and Tony was behind Serenai. He kissed the ladies good night and dozed off.

The next morning, Serenai woke up in the middle of Tony and Chuchie. She sat up for a minute trying to replay what happened the previous night. Tony felt her move and suddenly woke up. Good morning. He said as he got from under the cover. Morning! What happened last night? Serenai puzzled. We went to sleep. He said as he walked into the bathroom. So we didn't do anything? She questioned as she followed him into the bathroom. No, can I have a little privacy? He said as he tried to pee. Oh, sorry. She said as she walked out of the bathroom and shut the door. Chanel was still fast asleep.

Serenai sat down on the edge of the bed. So what time are you guys supposed to leave for the Bahamas? Serenai asked Tony walked out the bathroom. Three. He said as he got back into bed. What time is it now? He puzzled as he got comfortable. Nine thirty. She replied. Ok, wake me up at twelve. He said before getting back under the cover like a turtle.

I am so tired. Chanel said as Tony packed their luggage into the car. Baby, you can't be tired. Tony said as he closed the trunk. Chanel's mother stood behind the car. Ok, Mom we have to go. Tony said as he kissed his mother in law on the cheek. Have a safe trip honey! Her mother said as she back away from the car. Thanks Mom, I love you. Chanel yelled back.

REFLECTIONS

The flight was twelve hours. Four hours Chanel and Tony slept. Then the last eight hours the two talked about their future together. We are going to have five kids baby. Tony said staring at Chanel. Five? She puzzled. Yea! He responded. I'm only pushing out two. She said.

Welcome to the Bahamas. The man said as helped Chanel out of the car. Thank you, sir. Tony said as the man grabbed their luggage. The two were staying at Silver Springs Resort. It was a place Chanel had always wanted to travel to.

They spent their time waking the beaches, swimming, eating, and touring the sites. They even made love. Over the course the entire trip, they made it their mission to have sex everywhere they went. They felt like they were in heaven. They even went to a Toni Braxton concert while there. Chanel loved Toni. She wished she could sing like her.

It was so hot. It was at least a hundred degrees outside. Baby, I need water. Chanel yelled from the bathroom. She sat on the toilet defecating for an hour. The two had been on vacation now for a month. They decided instead of taking a week long honeymoon they would take a month. We have to go home baby. Chane yelled from the bathroom as she flushed the toilet and washed her hands. Ok, we will leave on Monday.

Monday came and the two headed back home. After another twelve hour flight, they were home at last. Chuchie was homesick and she was so glad to be back home. She immediately went to bed. She slept an entire week without waking. Tony thought she was dying.

When she finally woke, she went to the bathroom. As she was walking to the bathroom, her water broke. Tony! She yelled. Tony and Shaliah were downstairs watching a movie. Yes. He said as him and Shaliah raced up the stairs. My water broke. Jamal is coming. Chanel said as Tony and Shaliah reached the bathroom. They immediately packed her bag for the hospital and headed for the hospital.

After nine hours of labor, Jamal was born. Shaliah and Tony were the only two in the room when she delivered. Tony fainted twice. Shaliah held Chanel's hand as she pushed. Chanel checked out of the hospital two days later. She was now a mother and a wife. She was very happy.

Jamal was a handful. He cried every two hours. Tony and Shaliah cared for him the first two weeks of his life as Chanel recovered. She lost a lot of blood during the childbirth and was now suffering from anemia. After her recovery, she immediately began her motherly duties. She nursed every two hours and changed his diapers constantly. The Alexander family were living life.

I think we should take our marriage to another lével. I think we should try something different. Tony started. Like what? Chanel asked. We should explore new ideas and opportunities. Tony continued. I already told you I'm not going skydiving with you. Chanel said as she wrapped her hair up for bed. I want to have a threesome. Tony finished as he lay on the bed. What? She puzzled as she stared in disbelief. Baby, I feel like it could make our relationship grow stronger. He confessed. What do you mean? She asked now sitting on the bed. I mean I don't want to have to want for anyone or anything else unless it is with you. He spoke. Who would we even have a threesome with? She puzzled as she stared at him. I can ask Serenai. He spoke. Serenai! Why her? Chanel puzzled.

The only woman that crossed his mind was Serenai. He had dreamed of this moment since he had first met the woman. She was so beautiful to him. He fantasized about making love to her constantly.

Chanel thought about the idea. The two lovers she had in her life in the same bed, she thought. Deep inside, Chanel wanted to jump up and down like she had just won the lottery. She knew that if she were to say the wrong thing Tony would be a little skeptical. Then she remembered Serenai was a lesbian. Serenai hadn't been with a man in ages. The last man she was with was some guy named Rex. She slept with him just so she could get high. Chanel remembered how Serenai had told her it was the most unpleasurable experience she ever had.

Baby? She questioned him. Are you sure you want to do this? She asked as Serenai stood beside the bed. Yes I'll do anything for you. If this will make you happy, I'll do it. He responded as he stared at her. Serenai, are you sure you're ok with this? Tony quizzed the woman. I haven't been with a man in over ten years, but I think it will be ok. She replied as she eased on the bed.

REFLECTIONS

The house was very quiet. Jamal was spending the night with Shaliah. Chanel told her that Tony and her were going out on a date. The three had a threesome that night and loved it. Chanel woke the next morning and made her lovers breakfast.

Serenai and Chanel were closer than ever. They spent a lot of time together. Tony loved the life he was living. He and his wife shared their bed with Serenai every two weeks. It was perfect for him and her. They both craved Serenai's affection. She enjoyed being able to be there for the both of them. But she truly only yearned to be with Chanel. She was still a lesbian but was willing to make a sacrifice to keep Chanel happy.

Tony's cheating on you Chanel. Serenai spoke. Why are you always trying to ruin my relationship? Chanel raged. Serenai pulled an envelope from her purse and handed it to Chanel. What is this? Chanel puzzled. Don't open it until I leave. Call me if you want to talk. Serenai said before leaving the house.

Chanel tore open the envelope. It was filled with photos of Tony, Eliza, and Zach. In a few of the pictures, Tony and Eliza were kissing. One of the photos showed her whispering in his ear as he had his hand up her leg in a bar. One of the photos showed Tony entering Eliza's home as she had nothing but lingerie on. Then Chanel noticed an ultrasound. The ultrasound was dated for two months ago.

She couldn't believe her eyes. The man she loved was cheating on her with another woman. The woman was also having his child. Chanel was enraged. She made the decision to just continue living her life with her family.

Cancer

I'm sorry to tell you this Mrs. Alexander but you have stage one breast Cancer. What, are you sure Dr? Yes, the cancer has taken over twenty percent of your breast. If we start chemo as soon as possible we can stop it from taking over your immune system.

Tears welled up on her eyes. She knew that this would change her life. How would she tell Tony and her son? She immediately saw her funeral. The white roses she loved lay across her casket as she lied inside with her wedding dress on. The room was filled with sad faces.

Every time she was sad or angry, she made it her life to shop or go to the beauty salon. She decided to go to the beauty salon most of the time. The only woman she had ever let do her hair while she was in Virginia would be working. Trina Bradshaw was her favorite stylist. When Chanel first enrolled in college, she needed her hair done. In Florida, it was easy for her to find someone who could retwist her locks. Once in Virginia, finding a really good stylist was like trying to find a needle in a haystack. One day she walked into a beauty salon on the Southside of town and ever since she hadn't go anywhere else.

She walked into the salon with a weary look on her face. Chanel, Chanel! A woman yelled from the back. It was Trina. The woman was more radiant than ever. She was twenty pounds lighter and was as happy as she had won the lotto. Your hair is getting longer and longer each day child. Trina spoke as she signaled her to sit down in the chair.

What do you want done today? Trina asked. I just want to chop it all off. She said as a tear rolled down her cheek. Are you sure that's what you want to do honey? The woman asked her as handed her a few tissues to wipe her eyes. Yes, if my beauty is defined by my hair. Chanel said as she wiped her eyes. Hair doesn't define you Chanel. Your courage and will to keep going no matter the situation has gotten you this far. You are a beautiful woman with or without hair. And that man of yours is going to be by your side no matter what.

What am I going to do without you? Shaliah quizzed as she stared at the woman she loved. I just don't know what to do. Chanel cried. I can't tell my husband. He would be devastated. She finished. Shaliah had tears in her eyes. So no one else knows but me? She puzzled as she stared at the woman she loved. No. You're the first person I called.

I have three problems. I am gay, I'm African American, and a woman. And now this. They are going to destroy everything I love by getting to the people I love. Shaliah confessed. I can't lose you. If I lose you, I don't know what I would do. She finished. This is not the end of the world. Chanel yelled. You're right. It's the end of my world. Nothing will ever be the same. She spoke. Promise you won't tell a soul anything I just told you. Chanel said as she stared at Shaliah. I promise. Shaliah said before kissing Chanel on the cheek.

Shaliah was so hurt by the news. She didn't know what to do. She felt like she was the one who had Breast Cancer. She thought back to the life that Sheyana was living. Sheyana was pretending to have AIDS for the sake of her career. Shaliah didn't want to have to live a double life. She didn't want to have to explain any of her actions.

Chanel was everything to her. She really loved her. She decided she would have to be closer to her before she died. She arranged a press conference for the upcoming Monday. She called Tony and Chanel and invited them to the press conference.

I have called you all here today to make a special announcement. Over the past years, I have had the pleasure of travelling the world, meeting new people, and living an amazing life. I have seen many great days along with the casual weary days. I'm honoured that you have believed in me and continued to support me in my walks of life. I remember back to my youth when I was afraid to admit who I was but now I understand fear only kills dreams. I send my gratitude and condolences to all who will be upset by my decision. I have decided to withdraw my

candidacy as mayor. Forgive me for such a decision. But I feel my legacy will live on through the people. Thanks and God bless you all.

What? Why are you doing this? Chanel raged. I just have so much to focus on right now. I don't want to have to choose what is important. Shaliah said as Tony and Chanel sat across from the woman. If this is what you want, I support you whole heartedly. Tony spoke. I just don't understand why you would give up on your dreams. Chanel spoke with her arms folded. Ife isn't about politics. It's about the people you love. Shaliah responded staring at Chanel.

Tony's Broken Promise

Tony sat back in his chair and began to pray. He hoped that the last two years of his life could just go away. He now was a husband, a father to two beautiful sons, and an adulterous person. He promised himself and God after he was married he would no longer cheat on Chanel, but something inside of him longed for Eliza. He was in love with her. She made him feel whole. She filled the spots where Chuchie couldn't fit. She was willing and ready to do anything he asked her to do.

After he finished praying, he decided to go for a run. So he called up Shaliah and asked her to join him. She agreed to meet him at Lexington Park. He took a shower and went to meet the woman he always called his sister.

So how are you doing? I'm ok. Just a little stressed with everything going on. What's going on? I always trusted you with all my deepest darkest secrets. You are the only family that I have other than my parents and I love you Sha. Yea I love you too Tony. I've been having an affair with another woman. What? But I love Chanel with all my heart. So stop cheating Tony. Do you want to lose her? Of course not! I would die if I lost her or my son. Who is the other woman? Zach's mom. Wait you're sleeping with the mother of your child? Yes. I love her too. You love her! So why get married? I love Chanel as well. I love Chanel more. I just enjoy sex with Liza. She has no limits.

That's crazy Tony. I would never expect something like this from you. Shaliah said as the two stood talking.

I know I am going to call it quits tomorrow though. I just don't know how I am going to do it. Just end it. She's pregnant. What? Shaliah said spitting her water out. Yea, we had a mishap. A mishap is accidentally falling. You didn't fall. You laid down. Shaliah raged. I know it was a stupid mistake. He said as he drunk from his bottle. How long has this been going on? Since I found out I had a son. Wow! And now you going have a daughter and a son. How you going explain this to Chanel? I don't know. I just hope she forgives me.

Tony is cheating on you Chanel. Shaliah said. Tell me something I don't know. Chanel confessed. You know? Shaliah quizzed. Of course I do. I'm not stupid. He spends more time at that bitches house then he does eating my pussy. Wow! So what are you going to do? Shaliah quizzed. Continue being the happy wife I am. He's cheating and so am I. He told me he got her pregnant. I know. I think of it like this, if he wants to cheat let him cheat. As long as he continues to be a perfect father and supporter, I am fine. How did you find out? Shaliah quizzed. Serenai told me. She knows too? Shaliah quizzed. Yes. He thought because he slept with Serenai, she would betray me. Wait, what? Shaliah quizzed. I, Serenai, and Tony had a threesome. You let her into your bedroom? He wanted her to come in and I liked the thought. How many times did this happen? Like five or six. Wow! It was before I knew how I felt about you. Tony would never have a threesome with you. Fuck a threesome Chanel! I can't believe you kept this from me. Shaliah raged.

Don't tell Tony I know. Chanel started. What? Shaliah asked. I don't want him to know I know. Chanel finished. So you are just going to continue living this way? Shaliah asked as she stepped back from Chanel. What do you want me to do? Jamal needs his father. If we get a divorce, he will never spend any time with him. Chanel said as she moved closer to Shaliah. You are right. Shaliah replied. I know. I have to keep my family together for our child. If no children were involved, I would have left long ago. You still love me right? Chanel spoke. I don't know. I have to think about it. Shaliah said as Chanel kissed her.

The Truth Hurts

When she asked me if I was ready for love, I knew I had betrayed him. I knew that such passion I couldn't resist. I thought of how at home lied a man who loved me for who I was and cherished every second we spent together, but I would rather be in the arms of a woman. It hurt me deep inside to know I was hurting him. She touched my lips with the simplest touch and I yearned for more of her. I wanted to hold her and smell the beautiful cherry blossom in her hair. I wanted to taste her sensitivity as she screamed in ecstasy. I just wanted to hear her say my name in such a seductive manner that I would melt.

Wow! So you mean to tell me you loved a woman? He questioned with a confused look on his face. Yes. She was far more than exceptional. She was my every heart beat. She replied.

There was this one time when I almost left my husband for her. We had been having an affair for three years. She was the god mother of my son, Jamal. He was now three years old and she loved him like he was her son.

CHARLIE KAAR

Shaliah, how are you doing? Chuchie questioned as she answered the phone. I'm ok, just was thinking about what to get Mal for his birthday. Shaliah replied. I'm quite sure whatever you get, he will love. Chuchie iterated. You think so? Shaliah questioned. Of course! Your presence is more than enough for him. Chuchie reiterated. Ok. So are you free? I wanted to come and see you. Shaliah puzzled. Yes I am. You can come over and we can talk for a little while. Chuchie replied. Is Tony home? Shaliah asked. No, he won't be home until later this evening. He is out with his boys. Chuchie responded. Ok, good. I'll be there in a few. Shaliah cheered. Ok, see you soon. Chuchie expressed.

The door bell ring as Chuchie jumped out the shower and slipped into something sexy. She knew that she was in for a treat. She quickly rushed to the door. She peaked out the window and saw Shaliah standing there. Hi baby! Shaliah said as Chuchie opened the door.

Come in you sexy thang. Chuchie said as she pulled her in by her arm. Mal isn't here is he? Shaliah questioned as she walked into the door. No just you and I. Chanel expressed as she kissed the woman. The two went up to the bedroom and made passionate love.

What's your problem? Chanel questioned as the woman she loved showed her no affection. I can't believe I'm even doing this. Shaliah responded as she eyed Chanel. It's all your fault! You stole my heart and bed from my husband. You were the one who decided to let me in. Shaliah preached.

Tony is my everything. But your mind, your heart, your body, and soul, I yearn for each day and night. Chanel confessed. Oh Yea? You are the oxygen I breathe to survive and Tony is the water I drink to live. So why are you with him? Shaliah puzzled. I love him but I need you. Chanel answered as she got on top of the woman.

Tell him the truth. Shaliah said. No. I could never. You are his best friend. He loves you like you are his flesh and blood. Chanel iterated. I can't believe I have done this to him. Shaliah whined. I know that's why I can't tell him. Chanel reiterated. It's me or him. She declared as she began putting on her clothes. No. You can't be giving out ultimatums. Chanel raged. I can and am. She said as she walked out of the room. Chanel followed behind her. No don't go I love you. She yelled as Shaliah walked down the stairs.

REFLECTIONS

If you love me, you can't leave me. Chanel said as she stood between the front door and Shaliah. Chanel you left me a long time ago when you decided to get married knowing how I felt about you. I love you I do but I have a family and you know this. So what do you expect me to be your mistress forever or were you planning on inviting me into the bedroom with you and him? Shaliah raged. No it's not even like that. Chanel cried. I want a family too but I want it with you. I want children I want to come to you every day and hear you tell me how much you love me. Another has what I want to be mine. I can't take that asunder. You will never leave him for me. If you die tomorrow will you be celebrated? If you died tomorrow do you think everyone will know who you were and what you believed in? If you died tomorrow do you think you will be satisfied with the life that you have lived? Shaliah preached.

Baby I love you. Chanel spoke. Yea! I love you more. Shaliah expressed. You know I love you. Chanel said. Ok I'll think about it. Give me some time please. Chanel finished. Are you serious? Shaliah puzzled in disbelief. Of course I am. I don't know what I would do without you. You're my all. Chanel said as she rubbed Shaliah's right cheek. I love you Chanel. Don't you ever forget that! Shaliah spoke as she kissed Chanel's forehead. I promise I never will. Chanel replied. I love you. I'll call you later I have to go. Shaliah stated now opening the door. You promise you're going to call? Chanel asked she closed the door back. Yes. I'll call you later baby. Now give me a kiss so I can go. Shaliah said before walking out the door.

Farwell My Love

Shaliah went to meet with Ms. Devo. Her son had finally written back and Shaliah wanted to share the great news. She had got the letter earlier that day when she checked her mailbox. Ms. Devo, May I come up? Shaliah spoke through the box. Is there something wrong Ms. Pallavi? The woman spoke back a few seconds later. I have something for you. Shaliah finished. The woman let Shaliah in. Shaliah had to walk up three flights of stairs before she reached Ms. Devo's home. Hi my dear! Ms. Devo spoke as Shaliah walked into her home.

As Shaliah entered the house, she noticed how magnificent the house was. The ceiling had angels in robes all over it. The walls were decorated with the past ten presidents of the United States on the left side and on the right side there were pictures of prominent women. Oprah, Princess Diana, Cleopatra, Madam CJ Walker, Marilyn Monroe, Ella Fitzgerald, Susan B. Anthony, Hilary Clinton, Madonna, and Whitney Houston all were hung across the wall. The sofas were all white linen and the floors were white, plush carpet. It was both elegant and cool.

REFLECTIONS

Why don't you make yourself at home! Would you like anything to drink? Ms. Devo asked Shaliah as she showed her to the sitting room. Water would be fine. Please hold the tap. Shaliah expressed as she sat down. The woman disappeared into the house. Shaliah sat alone in the dimly lit room. The woman reappeared after a few minutes. Now what is it that you have for me? The woman puzzled as she handed Shaliah a bottle of water and a napkin. Shaliah drink a little of the water as Ms. Devo sat across from her. This is what I received in the mail today. Shaliah spoke as she pulled an envelope from her pocket. She placed the envelope on the table.

Ms. Devo stared at the words on the envelope for a second. It read:

Daniel Devo # 923165
701 Sanderson Road
Chesapeake, VA 23322

These words are to heal the soul of a child trapped inside of a grown man.

Ms. Devo quickly grabbed the envelope and ripped it open. Shaliah sat across in silence. Tears filled the woman's eyes as she read the letter. Shaliah thought of what the words could have said. She remembered very vividly what Ms. Devo had written to her son.

Daniel,

I know that you didn't want me writing to you or coming to see you, but this is my last time I promise. I have deep remorse in my heart for the actions that I displayed. I never thought in a million years that the one person I love whole heartedly could learn to hate me. It is very sickening to my soul to be able to speak to the only man I have ever come to love. I think back to all the mistakes that I made in raising you and I noticed where I went wrong. I never thought to ask you how you felt about your mother being a lesbian. It never struck a chord in me to consider that maybe you didn't accept this or wanted to acknowledge such a thing. I never bothered to ask you. I knew when I saw your face that day that I had betrayed you as a friend, as a counselor, and as a mother. My deepest fear was to lose you to the street life that I tried so hard to keep you away from, but I realized I lost you to a love that I couldn't help. The fact is I was scared for life by a man and I never wanted to experience such a pain ever again, but I didn't realize my pain caused you to suffer. I was hoping that I could teach my son to be a man who loved all for who they were but never understood that a man needs a man to teach him how to be a man. All I was supposed to teach you was the woman that you should love should be a good woman. All you saw was that I was in love with women. I apologize for not being the best mother I could be to you, but I must let you know I always have and always will love you no matter the time or any given circumstance. I hope that you accept my apology and respond to an old lady who is working on her last life. I also hope that you wish to acknowledge that I accept the blame for the shenanigans that took place between Kim and I. I want you to know that the girl was just a little lost and she needed someone to confide and she saw me as an exit. She was a brilliant woman and I always thought of her as a lesbian. She never struck me as being your wife and I know you may hate that I am saying this, but I have to be honest. I love you and will always love you. I know you may feel like I have betrayed your trust, but I want you to know I would never do anything to hurt you. Kim was a foul creature. I'm sure she probably hasn't come to visit you or even wrote you a letter.

I love you!!!
Jacqueline Devo

He says he forgives me. Ms. Devo cried as she put the letter down. What? Shaliah puzzled. You must read it my dear. The woman said to Shaliah as she moved to sit next to her. Are you sure you want me to read it. It's completely personal. Shaliah said as the woman handed her the letter. Nothing is personal when it comes to a miracle that you helped me to receive. The woman said as he wiped her eyes.

Mother, There are several things that a man must do before becoming a man. He must learn to be strong no matter the situation which may be at hand. He must know himself and love himself. He must be willing to give when can afford to give. He must learn to not be judgmental but to be open to all people. I never knew I wasn't a man until I read your letter. I have sat beyond these walls for such a long time now. I have begun reading, writing, and understanding on higher levels. I once thought that being a homosexual was wrong. I believed in my heart that if God created the heavens and the earth he must have created only things of pure quality. I believed that the world was only tainted because of the cruel and unusual ways of man. Now I am whole. I know and no believe in my heart the only way some people can be of any service to others is by listening and trying to understand what one may go through. Given the circumstance that is hand, I apologize. I apologize for trying for many years to make you be someone you truly were not. I apologize for not accepting you and trying to be the best son I could be to you. I apologize for the childish way I reacted. Kim was a woman that I was in love with. I wrote her several times and she hasn't responded yet. You are very right in your justification of calling her a foul creature. I do believe in my heart that she was the one who came onto you because as I remembered when I was younger you wouldn't date my football coach because of his relationship with me. And because of the fact that you were a lesbian. I want and need you to know I love you. I trust that you will forgive me for trying to kill you over a woman who never loved me. I almost lost a woman who has truly loved me unconditionally for the past twenty five years of my life. I will be coming home soon and also thank Ms. Pallavi for me. The guards said she said she came to make a dream come true and she truly has. I greatly appreciate her courage to step in and help out into strange situation. If she is a lesbian, you two have my blessing.

Love your only begotten son
Daniel

A tear fell from Shaliah's eye as she finished the letter. This was beautiful. Your son is very courageous. Shaliah said as she handed Ms. Devo the letter. I don't think you will be needing me anymore Ms. Devo. Shaliah began as she stared at the quiet woman. Maybe you are right. I know for certain I will never meet a woman of your cavalier . The woman said as she hugged Shaliah.

I must be going now. Shaliah said as she wiped her eyes. Yes my dear. Let's keep in touch my dear heart. The woman said as Shaliah headed for the door. Will do! I will be in touch. Shaliah said as she walked out of the front door.

I love her and I will never let anything come between us. She is mine. Pow Pow! The sound of the gun echoed through the silent, night air. Shaliah was hit twice, once in the stomach and one in the leg. She fell as her killer fled.

Three cop cars sat outside of Shaliah's home as Tony pulled up. He wondered what was going on. He parked his car behind a police car. Excuse me Officer what is going on? He asked as he walked up. Do you know the woman that owns this house? Yes she is my sister. What is going on? Tony puzzled. She was killed a few days ago. The officer spoke. Tony began to cry and stormed off. He went home to tell Chanel the horrible news.

Shaliah is dead Chanel. Tony said as a tear rolled down his cheek. What? Chanel puzzled in disbelief. She is dead. The police say she was found about three this morning by a dumpster. He continued. So this is why she hasn't been returning my calls and I thought she was mad at me. Chanel confessed as she sat down to keep herself from falling. What are we going to tell the kids? Chanel puzzled as she tried to hold back tears. That their auntie was killed. Tony cried.

Tony took the death of Shaliah the hardest. She was his little sister and he felt responsible for her. A part of him felt like if he would've been a little more focused on her she would still be alive. He had gotten so deep into his affair with Eliza that the two hadn't really hung out in a while. He blamed himself completely for her death. He thought of a million ways to cope with the lost of her.

She was truly a woman I was in love with. She will always have a place in my heart. Chanel thought as she sat in the room by herself still in disbelief. A void filled her heart now. She wondered why someone would kill such a selfless person. All she could think of was how Shaliah would do anything for anyone if she could.

REFLECTIONS

Today we are here to celebrate life. We are here in celebration of Ms. Shaliah Dakota Pallavi. This is not the end of the road; it is the opening of a gate. Jesus has called his angel to come back home. Her service was done and she is needed back alongside the king. We now will hear a selection from the choir. The pastor spoke.

The choir sang two selections. The first was Come Away with me by Norah Jones. A young girl led the song. It was a beautiful rendition. Every eye in the place had a tear in after she finished singing. Then the choir sung No Weapon by Fred Hammond. A male led this selection. This sung didn't receive the same outcome as the previous song.

That was very beautiful. God said no weapon formed against me shall prosper. There was a time when you were down and out, and God. I said God told you no weapon formed against you shall prosper. This is not goodbye, this is a hello. This is not a funeral; it's a home going celebration. We sing because we are happy, we sing because she is free. Free from persecution, free from the wicked one, and free from temptation. The audience cheered.

In the beginning God was the word and the word was God. I said God is the word and the word is God. If he said he would save you, he will save you. If he said you don't have to hurt no more, you ain't going hurt no more. Shaliah is not here with us anymore because God told her you don't have to hurt no more.

Now we gave time for some of her friends and family to reflect on her life. The pastor finished. Tony walked up to the podium. He had tears in his eyes. His eyes were blood shot red. He looked out at Serenai, then at Chanel, and then over at Shaliah's family. He walked towards her casket and touched it. The heavens are happy to have such angel. He whispered to his lifeless little sister.

I loved her like a sister. We grew up together not too far from here. We would support each other by trying to be better than each other. I played football and she played basketball. In my family, it was tradition for the males to play football. Shaliah's family had a great tradition as well. No one was allowed in their garden. The audience laughed. Shaliah was never the normal type of woman. She didn't like gardening, wearing heels, or anything that most women did. She liked everything that I liked. We argued about whether the Steelers were a greater team than the Patriots since we were twelve years old. I'm sure she knows why I always said the Patriots were better. The audience laughed. She was my best friend. Every time I wanted to do something different, I made sure it was ok with her first. My wife was approved by her. He spoke as he turned and looked at weeping Chanel. Shaliah told me that she was perfect for me, which I had already known. The audience laughed. I just want to say to the Pallavi family, Shaliah will always have a place in my heart. She will be missed by the entire Alexander family. She is gone but will never be forgotten. Thank you! Tony finished.

Thank you brother Alexander! The pastor spoke as he walked back to the podium. Now we will hear a few words from her best friend Chanel Alexander. He finished. Chanel walked onto the podium.

Shaliah was a great person. I remember when we first met. I immediately thought who is this woman. The audience laughed. She was beautiful on the inside and outside. She was the Godmother to my son Jamal and she was a great part of my family. I know that if she were here today we would probably be out doing something crazy. I was her bad influence. Tony would often tell me don't get her in trouble today. The audience laughed. She was more than a friend to me, she was a loved one. When I needed help with something and Tony didn't want to help, I called Sha Sha. Everyone that knew her called her Sha Sha. I found this really great poem that I know she is saying to us right now.

REFLECTIONS

Dear friends, I go, but do not weep,
I've lived my life, so full, so deep.
Throughout my life, I gave my best,
I earned my keep, I've earned my rest.
I never tried to be great or grand,
I tried to be a helping hand.
If I helped in a team,
If I helped on my own,
I was more than repaid
By good friends I have known.
And if I went the extra mile
I did it with pleasure,
It was all worthwhile.
If I brightened your path,
Then let it be,
A small contribution
From my loved ones and me.
But mostly I cherished the family I knew,
In a bond never-ending,
So precious, so true.
Now sadly I leave you, and travel alone,
Through the mystic veil
To the great unknown.
With such beautiful memories
That forever will be,
The way that I hope
You'll remember me.

The funeral was very still. No one moved or said anything as Chanel made her way back to her seat. She began to weep a little louder. Tony hugged her. He knew that his wife was traumatized. He wondered how Jamal would act.

The funeral ended and everyone went to The Alexander's house after. Everyone ate and talked about Shaliah. Jamal and Zach puzzled where their aunt was. Tony, Eliza, and Chanel tried to explain that she was in a better place.

Months had passed since the death of Shaliah. Serenai was there for Chanel as she coped with the lost. She would call and visit just to check on her. She became Jamal's new Godmother as well. She would take him out for ice cream, to the park, to school, and shopping. She was trying to fill the void of missing Shaliah. Larry and his family moved to Virginia to be closer to his best friend during his time of grief. Larry helped out Tony with his business. He would set appointments, make calls, and gain Tony new clients. He was being the best man he could be for Tony.

I want to move. Chanel said as she stared into Tony's weary eyes. I have some great news and bad news. She started. I am three months pregnant, but I don't want to continue raising our family here. This place is now a place of horrible memories for me. She finished. We have a house here and all my clients are here. Tony stated. I know but what about the safety of our family? She puzzled. Where do you want to move to? He asked. Anywhere outside of Virginia! She confessed.

Tony wasn't ready to move. He was happy in Virginia. His son, his mom, and his business were there. He thought of how the move could really affect him and his entire life. He had just convinced Eliza to move to Virginia. Now he was going to have to convince her to move to a new state. The thought of being without his son frightened him. He was his first born and he really wanted to be the perfect dad to Zach. He wondered how can I do this when Zach will be away from me.

THE BIG DECISION

The Alexander family moved to Fayetteville, North Carolina. Tony opened a new office and Chanel became a stay at home mom. Eliza and Zach moved there as well. They moved thirty minutes away from Tony and Chanel's house was.

After six months of being stable in the house, Casey was born. Serenai moved to Fayetteville to help out the family. She began sleeping with Chanel and Tony again. She felt like a great part of the family. She loved her life.

Chanel wondered what the next step in her life was. She had been living in Fayetteville for five years now with her family. She had lost so many love ones on the way. The one that stood out to her the most was Shaliah. All she wanted to do was make sure no one had forgotten about her. Shaliah was the only woman that inspired her to dream on a larger scale. She made her question whether the life she lived was truly a life worth living.

Chanel rushed through traffic on that blue afternoon. She was about to take on a challenge she had never dreamed of before. She pulled into the parking garage. She turned the car off and proceeded to the elevator. As she entered the elevator, a woman a child stood inside the elevator. The elevator smelled like a mixture of garbage, pee, and sour clothes. Chanel knew that she smelled the woman and the child. The woman was wearing an old jacket, a dingy pair of jeans, and a pair of beaten up sneakers. The child had spots all of his face. He looked like hadn't had a bath and or a meal since his first day of life.

CHARLIE KAAR

How are you doing? Chanel puzzled as she turned to face the woman. I'm going to speak with the mayor about a few things. I know this time he will see the light. The woman confessed as the child held onto her leg. What exactly are you going to see him about? Chanel puzzled. A tear fell from the woman's eye. This is his son. I met him a few years back. We started seeing each other. I got pregnant and was no longer able to work. He told me he would take care of everything. But then, I was blackballed from my job, my home, and was left with nothing but my son. His family didn't want to have a black son running around. Chanel was appalled. She couldn't believe what she was hearing.

Hi! Chanel spoke to the child. The boy hid behind his mother's leg. He looked like he was no older than three years old. He doesn't really talk. The woman said as Chanel tried to get the child to speak to her. The woman never got to speak to the mayor. Chanel didn't either. She was outraged. She thought how could a man with so much power be so selfish? How could one deny their one deny their own flesh and blood.

I think I am going to run for mayor baby. She said as Tony sipped from his drink. He stared at her for a second and began to speak. You can do anything you put your mind to. I have watched you deal with a lot and you truly are a remarkable woman. If this is what you want to do, I fully support you.

I would like to run under the Sawgrass campaign. The things that you guys believe in; I support wholeheartedly. Chanel spoke as the officials sat around listening. My best friend ran under this campaign and she got a lot done in the community. I think she wouldn't want me to do any other way. Chanel finished.

She was selected as the candidate for the Sawgrass Party. They believed in same sex marriages, abortions, free healthcare, free education, legalization of marijuana for recreational purposes, and lower taxes. It was exactly what Chanel believed in.

Election Day came. Chanel was not even recognized. No one knew who she was. All the voters voted democrat or Republican. Chanel lost by a landslide. Mayor Sean Banks won a second term. He ran under the Republican Party and had an enormous backing.

REFLECTIONS

Chanel took the lost very hardly. She thought it was because she was a black woman. Her family tried to cheer her up, but she never budged. Deep inside of her, she felt a feeling of rejection and betrayal. She thought society will never accept a woman as a leader, but as a cleanup woman and a wife.

Hi, Mrs. Alexander! A man spoke as Chanel walked out of the library. She spent a lot of her time in the library reading books and researching. Hello sir. Chanel responded a little startled. I saw your last campaign and I must say, you are a remarkable woman. The man spoke. I am a married woman. Chanel said as she put on her glasses. I am married as well. My name is Willie Trumont. He said as he reached his hand out to her. Ok, nice to meet you. She said as she shook his hand. I think you should run again. He continued. Come again. Chanel said. It wasn't the right timing. You are truly what Fayetteville needs. The man said as Chanel began walking to her car. You don't even know me. I'm just a stay at home mom. She said as the man followed behind her. You are very humbling. That's the reason you should run again. He said as they reached her car. Yea, ok. And who are you exactly? Chanel puzzled. I'm the president of the Democratic Party here in Fayetteville. He spoke.

Sir, I am honored but I have a family to raise. I have motherly duties to tend to. Chanel said as she unlocked her car door. Ma'am it wouldn't kill you to try. I know you have dreams of something more. Why not be more than you are? Are you afraid? He pushed. I'm not afraid. Like you said it's not the right timing. She said. I said it wasn't. Now it's your time. Be who you are Mayor Alexander. The man said. These people will never elect a woman as a mayor. It's preposterous. Chanel said. It's a new day and age. We all want the real deal now. Don't you? The man spoke. Here is my card. Just think about it. He said as he handed her the card. She took the card and got her car and drove off.

Two weeks had passed. Chanel thought about what Willie had said to her. She thought of she would be a great mayor. She called him up. He set up a meeting date for her to come to his office and talk.

CHARLIE KAAR

I've been thinking about it is all I'm saying. Chanel said as Willie sat at his desk. That's good to hear. He said. So what do I have to do? Chuchie asked as she sat down. You have to get the Democrats to believe in you. He said. How do I do that? Chanel puzzled. Submit an application and let me do all the rest of the work. He said as he handed her a thick envelope filled with papers. See you soon. He said as she walked out of the office.

Chanel woke up the next day with a massive headache. She woke to Casey running and jumping on the bed. Mommy wake up! She yelled and pulled as her mother slept. Not now. Chanel said as she stuffed her head under the cover and pillows that lied on her bed. But Mommy the mail man came. The child spoke. Ok! Chanel yelled as she crawled from under the comforts of her bed.

Where is Daddy? She asked as her and Casey made their way down the stairs. He's outside playing basketball with Jamal. The girl replied. Ok, what time is it? Chanel puzzled. It's three o' clock Mommy. The girl answered as they reached the kitchen. Chanel scanned the kitchen for food. A pot sat in the sink empty. Her stomach growled. Are you hungry Mommy? The girl asked her mother. Yes. I am going to eat some cereal. Chuchie replied as she grabbed some milk and a box of cereal.

Go play while Mommy eats. She told Casey. Ok. The girl replied before running off. Chanel sat at the table eating her breakfast. She noticed a gold envelope on the table. It said reply as soon as possible on it. She opened the letter and noticed it was an invitation. It was an invitation to a charity ball with the senator of North Carolina. The invitation instructed her she could only bring one guest. Of course it will be Tony. She thought. The event was being held in Charlotte.

Tony! Chanel yelled as she walked out on the pool deck. She walked pass the pool and to the basketball court where her husband, son, and daughter were playing basketball. Yes? He puzzled as she neared them. I got this invitation to go to a charity event. She said in between breaths. Tony walked over next to her. What is it? He puzzled as she handed him the invitation. We are going to a charity event the weekend of February 5th. She said. Ok, whatever you want baby. He said.

REFLECTIONS

Chanel was very excited. Tony purchased tickets to Charlotte the next day. The event was a weekend long event. The first night was Friday. It was just an introduction day. Guests from around the country gathered on this day to meet and greet one another. Saturday was an announcement day. The charities that would be funded from the fundraising were announced. Saturday was the most important night. It was the night money was collected at a very, elegant ball.

Hilary Clinton, you have my support. Senator Brown spoke as he shook the woman's hand. Splendid! Thanks for your support. Clinton expressed as the two sat down. With election right around the corner, I need a team like no other. She continued. I am very proud of the rebuilding you have done in this great state. Clinton said. It was all for better or worse. Brown joked as pulled a cigar from his pocket. There is a woman I want to have on my team. Clinton started. Who do you speak of? Brown asked as he lit his cigar. She is running for mayor for the city of Fayetteville. Clinton said. You mean Ms. Chanel Alexander? He puzzled. Yes. She will be the first woman to be elected in the city. I would like to meet Ms. Alexander. Clinton stated. She is here tonight. He spoke as he stared at Clinton. I will arrange it right away Mrs. Clinton. He said as he put out the cigar and headed out the door.

Chanel and Tony entered the ball wondering what would happen next. As they entered, they noticed many important members of the community were there. Condelezza Rice, Jimmy Kimmel, Al Gore, and The Schwarzenegger's were all in attendance. Chanel couldn't believe what was happening to her. Hilary Clinton, Michael Jordan, and Bill were in the same room as her. Tony and she were seated at the same table as Michael Jordan and The Schwarzeneggers. Everyone at the table was very familiar with Chanel. Michael told her she would win next time and Maria Shriver aid the women around the country were rooting for her.

The evening started off with an introduction given by the mayor of Charlotte. Senator Carlton Brown then gave a speech. Dinner was served after Senator Brown's speech.

You are needed at once Mrs. Alexander. A man said as he appeared. What am I needed for? Chanel puzzled. Mrs. Clinton would like to meet with you. He spoke. Who? Chanel asked. Ms. Clinton is waiting on you ma'am. He confirmed.

Chanel followed behind the man as he led her to the back of the establishment. She was a little worried about what she would say to the woman. Clinton was like an idol to her. She was the first woman to run for president and Chuchie found this to be so incredible. The man finally reached his destination. He opened the door and let Chanel inside. The former president of the United States' wife stood three feet away from her.

I am extremely honored to meet you Ms. Hilary Clinton. Chanel confessed as she walked closer to the former first lady. I saw your campaign a few years back and I thought to myself what a woman. Clinton said as she held her hand out for Chanel to shake it. A woman with your courage has nothing but my respect. So are you running in the upcoming election? Clinton continued as the two sat. I was thinking about running but I don't know if it is for me. Chanel took a breath as she spoke with the woman. You should never give up on your dreams just because they don't happen the way you want them to the first time. Clinton spoke. I know but I have a past that is full of shame and sorrow. I would like to spare my family the heartache. Chanel said.

Hilary Clinton stood from her seat and walked to the window. Mrs. Alexander, do you know what it is like to be a woman with a dream in this country? Clinton asked. What do you mean? Chanel asked with a perplexed look on her face. I mean do you ever sit back and wonder what it is like to have to give up on your hopes and dreams because of the simple minds of men. Do you ever think about what would have happened if Susan B. Anthony would have given up? Do you ever think of the way that women still receive seven times less pay for jobs that they perform well at compared to their male co workers? Do you ever think will your daughter have a woman as a role model who she can actually aspire to be like some day? Clinton puzzled as she stared at Chanel. If any of these thoughts have ever plagued you, you must run again and become someone who your children can actually say made a difference. Ms. Clinton finished as she sat back down.

I believe in you and I will support you all the way. Clinton spoke. But why me? Chanel puzzled. Because you have the courage of my mother. The woman never saw anything but a win. And if she ever loss, she said she had won experience. Clinton confessed. There is nothing you can't do Mrs. Alexander. Clinton spoke. Call me if you need me. Clinton finished as she handed Chanel her card and walked out of the room.

REFLECTIONS

Chanel went to find Tony. Hilary wants me to be mayor. Chanel said as Tony turned on the car. What? He puzzled before putting the car in drive. She wants me to run again. Chanel spoke as she stared out the window. How do you feel about that? She puzzled as she stared at her husband. I think that Mrs. Clinton said you're going to be the mayor, you have to. There is no fighting it. I know you believe in making a difference. The best is yet to come is what you always say right? Tony spoke. Yea but... But nothing maybe you are the best that you were talking about. Tony cut her off. It's written in stone. A great leader will lead us to the promised land. Tony finished. Baby, you know that's going to be Jesus. Chanel said as the two sat in the car. What are you so afraid of honey? He asked. I'm afraid of letting everyone down. First I was just afraid of letting my family down, but now Mrs. Clinton and Reverend Jackson are now all saying that I am the next best thing. I just feel like people are putting too much pressure on me. Chanel spoke. To whom much is given, much is expected. You have a lot, so you have to give a lot. You have to earn the respect and you have earned it.

I would like to submit my application to run for mayor under the Democratic Party. Chanel said as she stared at the committee. Everyone in the room suddenly got quiet. Are you sure? Willie asked. I am positive. Men have been running this city right into ground. Why not have a woman come in a clean the house? She joked. This is a very serious matter. This is not a beauty competition or a popularity vote ma'am. A young white man said as he stood. The man was Jim Thompson. I know this is about change and I promise I will change the city if I am elected mayor.

CHARLIE KAAR

Why have you decided to run under the Democratic Party? Your previous run, you ran under the Sawgrass Party. Willie puzzled as Chanel stood before them. As you all know, I didn't win the first election. I did a little soul searching and research of this city and I found out what I was missing. And that was the Democratic Party. Chanel stated. But why do you believe you would be an ideal candidate for the party? Willie questioned. I know that a lot of you are thinking I am just a woman with a little too much time on my hands, but I can assure I am truly capable of handling such a noble task. I am not here for the sake of any popularity contest; I am here to fulfill a legacy that was written a long time ago. I am here to make a difference in all the communities of this city. I am here to be your mayor. Chanel preached.

The men in the room started to speak. Simmer down now. Willie yelled. We will now hear from Mr. Jim Thompson. He finished. Jim Thompson had a rich family history involving men in politics. His father was the senator of North Carolina for six years, his uncle was the current senator of Virginia, and his great, great, great, great grandfather was Andrew Jackson.

What a woman! I applaud Ms. Alexander's effort and I commend her with great respect and gratitude. He said as he stared at his opponent. I am honored to be present before all of you great people today. I can't promise you that I will find any gold or oil mines, but I can promise you will see positive results. I know I may be a little old fashioned, but that's what gets the job done. Do we want to see an emotional woman handle our finances and legal matters? Of course not! My father would be very proud to see me as your mayor. Let's bring Fayetteville back! Jim cheered.

Chanel sat in disbelief about what she had just heard. Jim pulled the *woman can't do anything for me but and clean* act and it was very unpleasant to hear. She wondered if all the cheering the men in the room meant she stood no chance. She remembered the energy Shaliah had for Virginia Beach. She wondered if she was making her proud.

After all the votes have been counted, our decision is unanimous. It gives us great honor and privilege to announce this year's candidate. We see fit for the Democratic Party no other candidate than Ms. Chanel Alexander. Willie announced.

REFLECTIONS

Chanel couldn't believe her ears. She was selected as the Democratic Party candidate over Jim Thompson. It was an extreme victory. She knew she would have to work hard against the Republican's Party's very own Tom Maynard. He was a very conservative individual. He promised more jobs, better education, and the legalization of medical marijuana. He was white, a graduate from Yale University, and a man. All of this was a plus for him. Women were not recognized as being capable to run things in the city.

NO MORE SERENAI

We found the killer of your best friend. The voicemail said as Tony and Chanel played back their voicemails. They left the kids with Eliza and flew back to Virginia.

Once they arrived, they went to the police department. We are here about The Pallavi case. Tony said as Chanel stood behind him. The woman looked at them for a second and she told them she would be right with them. The two went and sat down on a bench across the room. They sat waiting for hours.

Hello, I'm Sgt. Alan Paine. I was handed this case after Sgt. Parks stepped down. A man said as he appeared before them. Nice to meet you sir. Tony said as the two shook hands. So you have details about the killer? Chanel said as she stood. Yes right this way. Sgt. Paine said as he led them through the office.

We have found a lot of clues to point us to the killer. Sgt began as they followed behind him. With recent tests, we have traced the saliva that was spit on her back to the killer. He continued. The new age of technology helped out a great deal with this one. He finished as they reached his office.

REFLECTIONS

Do you know of a Serenai? He asked as they all sat down. Wait what? Tony asked a little confused. Serenai couldn't have done this. Chanel said in disbelief. The bullet that was found in the victim's intestines were registered to her. She purchased the gun seven months before the murder happened at a local gun shop and the saliva was hers as well. Sgt. Paine said as he showed the couple the paperwork. My team is trying to find her whereabouts right now. Would you happen to know who she is? Sgt Paine continued. Of course we do. Chanel said with a tear in her eye.

Two days later Serenai was transported from North Carolina back to Virginia Beach. Will we get to see her before she is locked away? Chanel puzzled. If you must. Sgt. Paine said as he wrote in his folder.

Serenai sat in a holding room. Chanel couldn't wait to see her. She wanted her to feel the same pain she felt. She wanted her to be executed for the death of her best friend. Tony said he didn't want to see her. He couldn't believe Serenai would commit such a crime. He thought of how Serenai had attended Shaliah's funeral. She cried as if though she had missed her too he thought.

Don't say a word. I can't believe you. You backstabber! She was everything to me and you know it. Is that why you killed her? Did you think that she was going to come in between us? Were you jealous of our relationship? I let you around my family. I shared my soul with you. I gave my all to you. It wasn't enough. You are the worst human being ever. I can't believe I ever loved you. Everyone tried to warn me about you. I hope they give you the death penalty. You were supposed to love me not hurt me. You are a despicable person who will rot in hell for eternity.

Serenai sat silently in handcuffs as Chanel raged on and on. She spit in the woman's face and stormed off. Chanel and Tony immediately got on a plane and flew back home. Chanel had hated Virginia because she thought it was dangerous; when in reality it was her very own Serenai.

Once home, Tony and Eliza explained that Serenai wasn't going to be in their lives anymore to their children. The kids didn't understand. They thought Serenai loved them and she would never leave them. Serenai was sentenced to life in prison without parole.

A few weeks later, Chanel had a debate against Tom Maynard. Willie, I don't think I'm ready. Chanel said as the two rushed into the auditorium. What do you mean? We made it too far to give up now. He said. Ok, but maybe it's a sign. Chanel said. A sign for what? You already defied the odds. You are here and you are going t rock. He said. Now go give them what they want. He said as he left her.

Today we witness a debate from our candidates for mayor. We have Chanel Alexander under the Democratic Party and we have Tom Maynard under the Republican Party. Each candidate will be given fifteen minutes to answer each question. After time is up, the bell will ring to let you know your time is up. We will begin with a coin toss to see who will be first. John Cartwright spoke. Call it in the air Mrs. Alexander. He said as he threw the coin up. Heads! Chanel yelled. And it is heads. Who will be going first Mrs. Alexander? Cartwright puzzled. Mr. Maynard will go first she said as she walked away.

How do you feel about taxes? Taxes are fine by me. As long as they are equal. The constitution says that all men are created equal. How can we be equal if I have to pay more taxes because I decided to get a job and work while lazy bums decide to sit at home and live off the welfare system? I believe that we all should pay an equal tax. One flat tax rate should be used across the board. That would be justifiable. Tom spoke.

Taxes are not a way to take from the rich. Taxes are ways and monies that families that never had the opportunity to go to college and get an education so that they could have a better job survive. Are we to say that because you and I went to college and now make seven figures that a mother and a child should starve because a mother has to stay home and care for her child? Are we to say that because a person is disabled and unable to work they shouldn't eat? Of course we aren't to say such a thing. What we as Americans should be saying is how can we help make life better for these citizens? Chanel spoke.

How do you feel about abortion? Cartwright asked.

REFLECTIONS

The debate over whether or not abortion should be a legal option continues to divide Americans long after the US Supreme Court's 7-2 decision on Roe v. Wade declared the procedure a "fundamental right" on Jan. 22, 1973. Many of these woman seeking abortions are troubled. They seek abortions due to many different reasons. With male counterparts shaming and slandering these poor women, what is one left to believe? Poor women must bear and raise alone children they cannot afford to bring up. Teenagers are to bear children they are not emotionally prepared to deal with. Women who wish for a career must give up their dreams, stay home, and bring up babies; and, worst of all, condemning victims of rape and incest to carry and nurture the offspring of their assailants. Legislative prohibitions on abortion arouse the suspicion that their real intent is to control the independence and sexuality of women. Chanel spoke.

A newborn baby is surely the same being it was just before birth. There's good evidence that a late-term fetus responds to sound including music, but especially its mother's voice. It can suck its thumb or do a somersault. Occasionally, it generates adult brain-wave patterns. Some people claim to remember being born, or even the uterine environment. Perhaps there is thought in the womb. It's hard to maintain that a transformation to full personhood happens abruptly at the moment of birth. Why, then, should it be murder to kill an infant the day after it was born but not the day before? It's murder no matter which way you look at it. Tom spoke.

How do you feel about the war on drugs? Cartwright asked.

There a great deal of crimes that are seen as heinous. The most outrageous crime is killing your fellow brothers and sisters. By selling drugs, we lose our citizens. The war on drugs is needed to stop the pollution of our communities and the dropout rate of our kids. Babies are dying because of malnutrition caused by their junkie parents. Kids are selling and using drugs instead of attending school. We have to clean up the mess that we as citizens have made. Tom spoke.

The war on drugs is a problem throughout many communities. The assumption that most urban areas are where the war on drugs should take place has caused a rising death rate. Students going to school are being killed by police officers. Police officers are locking away innocent young men. And the biggest drug use problems are coming out of suburbia. The fallacies that are being bestowed by the constant revival of the war on drugs is polluting our urban youth to believe the only way out is through not going to school so they want be killed on the way. The war on drugs has to be stopped. Chanel spoke.

What are you plans as far as the high unemployment rates? Cartwright asked.

I will create more jobs. Tom talked for fifteen minutes. The crowd cheered. He was quite intelligent Chanel thought. If she wasn't running she probably would have voted for him. Tony even went as far as saying Tom was very smooth. His way of handling business was like a snake. He eased his way to you then caught you like prey until he struck.

I will bring in new companies to help decrease the unemployment rate. Chanel spoke for ten minutes. She really hadn't researched the topic of unemployment. She just knew that if she were elected she would find some way to bring more jobs. This was what she really wanted.

What are your primary goals?

Once I am elected mayor, I will restore Fayetteville. I will make this city a place to live without fear. I will create more jobs and I will create stimulus packages to help failing home and business owners. I will be an advocate for each and every community. There will be light shined on all the prevailing problems. No issues will go unresolved. The demand for more support from the leaders in Fayetteville will diminish. There will be a new support system known as The A List. The mayor's office will be open for any questions and concerns that anyone may have. If any citizen of this beautiful home of mine is down, I will do whatever is in my power to help. Chanel spoke.

REFLECTIONS

Tom took a deep breath. He seemed to be a little overwhelmed by the questions. He thought of what was to come. He remembered his father's words and considered only being the best he could be. The man knew that it was now or never. He thought back to his younger days watching his family be a voice of the people. He looked out into the audience and began speaking.

As an official, it is surely our duty to be the voice of the people. I have heard the people and I know that we all are looking for the real McCoy. We no longer want to sit back and watch poverty and crime strike us like a storm in the night. As your mayor, I will not only be the best I could be but also the knight in shining armor to save what is dear to my heart. I will enact legislation like no other city has seen. I will create a prosperous economy throughout this land. I will invite more business owners to this community. I will implement more educational programs to help stimulate the graduation rates. I will create a place of reform for the mothers of children who are afraid to take on motherhood. I will cancel the wage of war that has been waged on the baby mothers. I will clean up communities with the continuous support of the war on drugs and poverty. I will be your prime time leader citizens of Fayetteville.

The audience cheered as Tom finished his speech. Tony sat in the audience wondering how this debate would play out. He thought of how so many people were supporting both his wife and Tom Maynard. He felt like the debate was at a tie and depended on the closing statements.

Now we hear the closing speeches from each candidate. We will start with Mr. Tom Maynard. The crowd cheered as he walked back out onto the stage.

CHARLIE KAAR

I Live For Her

REFLECTIONS

I would like to thank you all for coming here today to witness such a debate between myself and Mrs. Alexander. But the truth is only you know what you need. I have been around the city and in the many different communities and I have seen it fit that, we all need a man to come in and set things straight. The good book speaks of man being the head of every household. Well, Fayetteville is my household. I have lived here since the day I was born. I left for college to study politics at Yale and I returned home. I returned home with a vision of love and empowerment. I feel that I am empowered to show love and respect to my family here in God's great city of Fayetteville, North Carolina. I feel empowered to acknowledge that this is a time of rejoice and replenishing. We need to replenish our city with sound minds and hearts. This is not a time to have to think about what this city can do for us; this is a time to think about what we can do for this city. I have walked the streets these past few months, and I have seen what this city is missing. It's missing a heart. The city has been tormented and filled with lies and deceptions for too long. I am sick of going to the store and not being safe because someone wants to rob me. I am sick of going to the movies and being harassed for spare change. I am sick of being unsafe and unrighteous in my own home. That has to stop and has to stop now. The heart that this city is missing is a heart filled with love, respect, communication, and proper training. The heart that this city is missing is not like any other you have ever come to know. This heart of mine is the heart of tradition as old as this great city. This heart of mine is the reaping and sowing of a man that will never be forgotten. This heart of mine is the heart of a veteran who has fought to defend our great home, this heart is of mine is of pure North Carolina blood. Are you brothers and sisters of mine ready for this heart of mine? If so, help me bring Fayetteville back to life!

The crowd cheered as Tom walked off the stage. It was now Chanel's turn. She thought of the hard work and dedication Shaliah once had. She knew that her speech would be the defining moment for the election. She walked to the podium and began to speak.

There a lot of great things that brings us together. One of those things is always the election of your leaders. I am very proud to say that I am here under the Democratic Party today. I speak for the democrats around the city and I say that this is the time that you have all been waiting for. There are a few things I must address before we can go any further. First off, let me start by addressing the slanders that have been displayed upon me and my family. I may not be an Ivy League graduate, I may not be a direct descendant of any politicians, and I may not be a man but one thing I am not is an illiterate, self righteous, baby mama. That is by far the worst thing anyone could ever think of me. I graduated from college, I was married my senior year in college, and I have two beautiful children with my husband. I believe that makes me a wife, a mother, and an educated African American woman. While I was a child, I did childish things. I'm not the person I once was anymore. I have learned that in life I will face many obstacles. I have also learned that no one is perfect and that if I expect anyone or anything to be perfect, I will always be at a loss. There are several things that I could tell you citizens that I am going to do, but I am not. There is absolutely no way in hell, that I can promise I will be Mother Teresa or Mother Mary. I will not even say that I will be the best for the job. I will say whatever I have the support of the city in doing, I will do. I will create more jobs and I will be proactive in each and every community. I will be the woman, God willing, to restore this city.

Do you think Shaliah is smiling right now? Chanel whispered in Tony's ear as she hugged him. I think she is crying right now because you are living for her. He said as he kissed her cheek. I think she will be even more proud when the first African American female mayor is elected. Tony finished.

Chanel Alexander I believe you to be a very promising young woman. I hope this election doesn't separate us. Tom spoke as he walked into the rom. Thanks so much! Chanel said unmoved. She just wished she could go home and sleep.

Three days later votes were casted. The city was a red, white, and blue for three entire days. Early voting wasn't as busy. People wore shirts with her face plastered on them. They held signs with her name all over them. Kids wore buttons with her name on them. The LGBT community created a flag with her name on it. Tom and Chanel both prayed for the best.

REFLECTIONS

Three days after the election, the results were to be announced. Americans across the country watched and waited to see what happened. Tom and Chanel stood waiting for the results to be said at the Grand Stony building in the auditorium. It was the first time an African American woman ran for the mayor's seat in a very racist place.

We are proud to announce this year; we have seen more voters than ever before. The citizens of Fayetteville, North Carolina have voted. The votes have been counted and for the first time in the history of the city, we have an African American woman as mayor. The man said.

Tom shook Chanel's hand as the crowd cheered. Chanel kissed her husband and she hugged her children. She couldn't believe the news. She was the first African American woman to be mayor in the city of Fayetteville, North Carolina.

Hilary sat watching the election. She shed a tear. That woman is a very courageous woman. She said to Bill as the two watched the television. I'm going to be on Collin tomorrow. Bill said as he stood from his chair.

In a very promising election this year, we are just hours away from meeting the first African-American woman to become a mayor of Fayetteville, North Carolina. Collin announced. Bill, how do you feel about such a turn of events? Collin questioned. We have seen a lot of great things happen over the past few years. This is what our country needs. Bill stated. And what exactly is that Mr. Clinton? Collin quizzed. More women in office! The crowd cheered as Bill finished. Your wife is actually an endorser of the Alexander campaign. Collin confirmed.

Right, it's truly remarkable how two of the strongest women in America can come together for a greater purpose. Clinton expressed. Do you think that Mayor Alexander will fold under pressure or will she show up and perform? Collin asked. I have had the pleasure of getting a chance to sit down on several different occasions to talk with Mrs. Alexander and I know she is the one that will get the job done. She has so many plans to bring the city back and I know she will be successful at them all. The crowd cheered as Clinton finished.

What do you think was the defining factor in this election? Collin puzzled. For me, it was the agility, the charisma, and the knowledge that she had. Clinton finished. Hillary once called Mrs. Alexander the young Hil, do you think that comparison is true? Collin quizzed the former president. Of course! Mayor Alexander has been a hard worker since she was younger and she knows how to inspire individuals to be all they can be as well. There is no other person that we can compare to my wife other than Mayor Alexander. Clinton finished.   Thanks for being here tonight Mr. Clinton as we experienced the breaking of an old chain. Collin stated. Thanks for having me. Clinton affirmed. We will be right back after this. Collin declared.

Great job! Collin stated. I love the show man. Clinton said as he shook Collin's hand. It's always a pleasure to have you here. Collin iterated. Thanks Collin. Bill left the stage. He entered his dressing room. And he turned on the television, he wanted to see the woman his wife had believed in just walk across that stage.

Welcome back. We are just minutes away from the initiation ceremony of Mayor Alexander of Fayetteville. The coverage of this is amazing. Citizens nationwide have their eyes glued to televisions to witness a decent moment in history. Collin started. How is city of Fayetteville right now Tom? Collin finished. You know the city hasn't been still since the mayor was elected. The town is overpopulated with tourists who drove, flew, swam, and hitch hiked all the way here just to be near such a remarkable event. Tom Shaw reported. Do you think Mayor Alexander is astounded by the past weeks turn of events? Collin asked. Of course, she has been in and out meetings since Election Day. She has also spent most of her time away from her family according to an inside report. She wanted to treat it as if it was her wedding day; she was not to be seen until the ceremony. Tom finished. Thanks Tom. Collin said.

"I do solemnly swear that I will faithfully execute the office of mayor of Fayetteville, North Carolina, and will to the best of my ability, preserve, protect and defend the laws of this land."

As you just saw Mayor Alexander was just sworn into office. Four years to come. See you next time on Collin Tonight. Collin said as the show ended.

REFLECTIONS

I stand here today humbled by the task before us, grateful for the trust you have bestowed, mindful of the sacrifices borne by our ancestors. I thank the mayors before me for the services to our city, as well as the generosity and cooperation he has shown throughout this transition. On this day, we gather because we have chosen hope over fear, unity of purpose over conflict and discord. On this day, we come to proclaim an end to the petty grievances and false promises, the recriminations and worn out dogmas, that for far too long have strangled our politics.

I AM WHO I AM

The light gleamed from the ceilings as the two continued talking. Chanel felt like she had just experienced a manifestation. She felt like a weight had been lifted off her shoulder. She had kept all this inside of her for so long and now everyone would know the truth.

So no one knows that all of this has taken place? He puzzled. No one knew about all of my lifestyle choices other than Shaliah. She was the only person I ever revealed everything to and now you. Chanel expressed. Are you not afraid of what people may say about you? Mr. Reed puzzled. I think that people will say a million things about me, but I just want my story to be told. She replied. Do you pride yourself on all the things you have done Mrs. Alexander? He questioned. I believe that there was a purpose in all the things that I have done, seen, or maybe even heard. I am proud that I am now at a place where I feel like I can let the world know in on the truth. Chanel preached.

Is there anything else you want anyone to know? He asked. Yes. I just say this to all people, not just Americans, or African Americans, take pride in who you are. Never ever let someone tell you that you will not be who you want to be and never give up on your dreams. She started. Don't you think that is a little cliché to say? Reed puzzled. No. I used to think the same exact way. Now I see why many years ago a woman said to me, if you die tomorrow will you be celebrated? If you died tomorrow do you think everyone will know who you were and what you believed in? If you died tomorrow do you think you will be satisfied with the life that you had lived? I never got to answer that woman but if she were here today I would tell her I will be celebrated centuries after I am gone. They will know my name not because the words they heard of me but because of what they saw me do.

REFLECTIONS

This has been a very promising interview for me Mrs. Alexander. Mr. Reed began. I hope that you have everything you need for your article. Chanel said as she walked Mr. Reed to the door. I have a perfect article about one the greatest women to ever live. He finished. Thank you and farewell. Chanel said as the man walked out of the door. She watched him put his things in the car and drive off before she shut the door.

Three months later the interview between Chanel and Mr. Reed was published. Around the country it was a bestseller. Fans flocked to read about the first African American Mayor of Fayetteville, North Carolina. The issue covered everything everyone wanted to know about the woman. They wanted to know who she was and how she had came out of nowhere and made such an impact. Many couldn't believe what that were hearing or reading.

Tony read the issue as well. He was appalled by all the things he read. He had never known about his wife's infidelities, Cancer diagnosis, or that she knew of his infidelities. All the things they were trying to hide from each other, the entire world now knew. Chanel! He yelled from the bedroom. Yes Hun. She replied as she walked into the bedroom. I just read the article and I don't know what to say. He confessed as she sat next to him on the bed. There is nothing you can say. I have made a lot of mistakes and so have you. She expressed. But how could you... How could I what? She cut off. How could I confess about my husband's infidelities with his baby mother? How could I confess about a life that I shared with your best friend that you never knew about? The question that you should be asking is how could I have stuck by your side after you got her pregnant while you were married to me. Chanel raged.

I am so glad you invited me. Chanel spoke as she gave the woman a hug. I am very delighted to see you as well dear. Clinton expressed as she sat down. I want you to come and visit Fayetteville. Chanel begged. Ok. I will come only if you promise that I will get to see the kids. Clinton joked. I was recently contacted with many different offers to do a book. Do you think I should do a book? Chanel asked Clinton. Why not? They have books on serial killers and monkeys, why not have a book on a woman like you. Clinton responded. What should I say in the book? Chanel puzzled. Tell the truth. The world doesn't care to hear a lie anymore. Just tell your story honey. Now I have a press conference to get to. Clinton finished as she put on her glasses. The two said their goodbyes as the women left the room.

Six months later, Clinton kept her word. It was a very cold day in Fayetteville. Clinton arrived two days before the press conference. She did a few meet and greets around the city. The day of the press conference she showed up ready to rock. What do you need me to do Mrs. President? Chanel joked as the woman prepared her speech. Give me an introduction I will never forget. Clinton replied. That's fine by me she said as she walked to the auditorium. The crowd cheered as she stepped on stage. She waved and began to speak:

Citizens of Fayetteville,

REFLECTIONS

With the tremendous delight that has overcome me, I stand here today as the voice of the people. I speak for the black communities, the white communities, the Jewish communities, the Muslim communities, the Christian communities, and the LGBT communities, and I say thank you. I want to thank you all for helping me reduce the crime rate, the poverty rate, the unemployment rate, the high school dropout rate, and the loss of home ownership rate. I could not have done this without you all backing and supporting these noble causes. And for those of you who questioned whether I was truly capable of such a task, please check my facts. I thank you all for giving me not one but two chances. This term is going to be even better than my first one.   For those of you who do not accept that I am who I am, I know a few very prestigious individuals who do. A few of them sit, sleep, walk, pray, and eat beside me each and every day. Then there is this one person who has been an avid supporter of mine since I first decided to run for mayor. She is an extremely dedicated woman. She too has a past filled with turmoil, confusion, and happy days. I have known this woman personally over a decade now and I must say she deserves much respect. She has been a great mentor and role model for me and many young women across the world. I cannot define this woman by her skin color, her hair, or by the tremendous amount of glasses she may wear, but I can tell you she has a beautiful soul. This woman who I present before the city of Fayetteville, North Carolina, is such a hard worker. It is a great honor and a privilege to introduce you all to **President Hilary Clinton.** Chanel finished as she hugged the woman.

www.ingramcontent.com/pod-product-compliance
Lightning Source LLC
Chambersburg PA
CBHW031311280626
47169CB00017B/1191